SEDUCTIVE SECRETS - BOOK 2

SECRETS OF THE HEART SERIES

ELIZABETH ROSE

ROSESCRIBE MEDIA INC.

TO MY READERS

Secrets of the Heart is a series about the daughters of the bastard triplets from the Legendary Bastards of the Crown which is followed by Seasons of Fortitude. This series can be read as standalone books, but if you prefer to read them in chronological order, I have listed the series below.

Legendary Bastards of the Crown:
 Destiny's Kiss – Series Prequel
 Restless Sea Lord – Book 1
 Ruthless Knight – Book 2
 Reckless Highlander – Book 3

Seasons of Fortitude Series:
 Highland Spring – Book 1
 Summer's Reign – Book 2
 Autumn's Touch – Book 3
 Winter's Flame – Book 4

Secrets of the Heart Series:
  Highland Secrets – Book 1
  Seductive Secrets – Book 2
  Rebellious Secrets – Book 3
  Forgotten Secrets – Book 4

Enjoy!

     Elizabeth Rose

CHAPTER 1

ENGLAND, 1386

"Willow Douglas ye're stealin' from a dead woman!" Morag exclaimed as Willow snatched up her late mentor's ring and bracelet and slammed shut the wooden box.

"I am not," Willow sniffed, replacing the box on the dusty shelf of the cottage. "Imanie would have wanted me to have these things. She said so at one time, but just never had the chance to give them to me before she died. I need them since the earl's annual autumn festival starts tomorrow and I want to look my best. Now that Fia is back in Scotland, there will be more men who will want to dance with me. The better I look, the more enticing I will be to the visiting barons and earls."

"What ye mean to say is that ye want all the men to

yerself," spat Morag. Her long, wavy, golden hair reached all the way to her elbows. Morag and her sister, Fia were raised in Scotland, but the rest of the cousins grew up in England. The girls were the daughters of the triplets of the late King Edward III. Their fathers were known as the Legendary Bastards of the Crown.

"The earl already told me that he has invited at least a dozen single, titled men who have requested to meet me," boasted Willow. "He also said some of them are bringing gifts. Perhaps the gifts are for me. I wouldn't miss this for the world."

"No gift is enough to convince me to dance with men I don't know," grumbled Maira from the doorway.

"Me, either," added Morag.

"Good," said Willow flipping her long, flowing hair over her shoulder. She, by right, should wear it tied back, in a braid, or under a wimple. But Willow liked to leave it loose. "If you two refuse to dance, there will be more men for me to choose from. I heard that Baron Chester of Ashington, as well as the rich Sir George of Canterbury, will be coming to Rothbury. So will the very handsome Sir Bedivere of Gaunt. And to top things off, Earl Stanley Alnwick is passing through on his way to see the king, with a ruby for King Richard that is supposedly the size of his hand!" Her eyes opened wider. "Can you imagine how that stone would look hanging from a chain around my neck?"

"Willow, that's a gift for the king, not for you. You live in a dream world," Maira scolded.

Willow met her cousin in challenge. "Better a dream

world where I'm adorned with expensive jewels and fine silks and surrounded by handsome men, then the empty, sad lives you two live. Now, hold the lantern higher, Morag. I don't want to stumble in the dark. I have to look my best tomorrow, and I can't fall and become bruised."

They were in a small cottage in the late Queen Philippa's secret garden that had at one time been Imanie's home. Imanie was the old woman who mentored the girls in secret these past few years. Willow and her cousins, Fia and Maira, had been chosen by the queen to join a secret group of strong women called the Followers of the Secret Heart. Morag was naught but a tagalong. But before Imanie passed away, she made Morag a member as well.

"Morag's right," said her cousin, Maira. She held her sword in one hand and a lantern in the other. "You shouldn't be taking things that aren't yours. I can't believe you convinced us to be a part of this deceitful act."

"Fia always said that Willow could convince the king himself to listen to her and act on her suggestions if she so wanted." Morag made a face.

"It's my talent," said Willow proudly. "Imanie said I was good at persuasion and there is nothing wrong with using my skills to bring about certain outcomes."

"Well, I dinna remember Imanie tellin' ye that ye could have her jewelry," Morag complained.

"Imanie has been dead for over a year now," Willow reminded her. "If I don't put her things to good use, they'll only be stolen by bandits sooner or later. I'm actually surprised no one has ransacked the house or garden by now."

"That's because no one kens about this secret garden but us," Morag told her.

"That's not true," answered Willow, taking the second lantern from Morag and heading to the door. "Branton knows."

"Willow's right," agreed Maira, still keeping her watch at the door. "Plus, don't forget some of the castle guards know about it now, and so does Laird Alastair MacPherson."

"Alastair isna goin' to steal anythin'. He's Fia's husband now." Morag had seemed lost without her sister for the last year, ever since she married and moved to the Highlands. Willow almost felt sorry for her since she was Scottish, being raised in England. She was also the youngest of the girls. But even with Fia gone, Morag continued to be a pest. Possibly even more so now.

"You are so immature, Morag." Willow stopped for a moment to put on the ring and bracelet and then pushed past the others out the door.

"I'm no' immature," spat Morag, following her out into the garden. It was night, and a full moon shone down, illuminating the grave of Imanie. The large wooden cross they'd constructed in her honor marked the spot. A dark shadow from the head marker covered the ground behind the grave while the moon bathed the cross in an eerie glow.

Alastair had buried the old woman after she dropped dead from a bad heart last year. The girls all missed their mentor tremendously. Without her, they were the last of the members of the Followers of the Secret Heart. Or at least, they didn't know of any more members since Imanie kept that a secret.

"I'm the same age as ye, Willow. I'm seven and ten years of age now," Morag reminded her.

"I'm closer to eight and ten than you are, and I still say you are immature." Willow felt as if sometimes Morag was only there to irritate her and to cause trouble.

"Stop it," said Maira, scanning the grounds, always watching for intruders. She gripped the sword her father had given her, ready to use it if need be. Her father, Rowen, was a strong warrior and, at one time, a pirate. Maira was a small girl with blond hair, but her courage and her rebellious attitude made her seem larger than life. "We need to hurry up and get back to the castle before Lord Beaufort realizes we're gone."

"Too late," came a voice from the gate of the secret garden. Branton, the earl's page who was hoping to become a squire, rode into the garden atop a horse. "The earl sent me to fetch you."

"He kens we left?" asked Morag.

"You told him," Willow accused the boy.

"Of course, the earl knows, and I didn't tell him," Branton answered with a puff of air from his mouth. "Everyone knows that you three sneak off here whenever you can. Who could miss three noisy girls leaving in the middle of the night?"

"It's not the middle of the night," Maira corrected him.

"The sun set only a few hours ago, so stop exaggerating, Branton."

"All right, so it isn't," agreed the boy. "But it is dark and cold and looks like it might even snow. The earl sent me to protect you three." Branton sat tall atop the horse, running his hand over the hilt of his new sword.

"Protect us?" asked Maira, handing her lantern to Morag and pushing her sword into the sheath attached to her back. "You honestly think you can protect us better than I can?"

"Of course, I can. I'm a man." Branton's smirk in the moonlight wasn't missed by any of the girls.

Maira reached up and, in one motion, pulled Branton off his horse and to the ground. He landed flat on his back with the air knocked from his lungs. Before he could even reach for his sword, the tip of Maira's dagger rested under his chin. "Think again," she told him. "You're only a boy of five and ten years of age. That's a far cry from a man."

"That wasn't funny, Maira!" Branton jumped up, pushing her away. His face became red with embarrassment. "What are you girls doing in the garden this late anyway?"

"Willow's stealin' Imanie's jewelry," Morag blurted out, never knowing when to keep her mouth shut.

"I'm not stealing anything. I'm . . . borrowing it," said Willow, holding the ring up in the moonlight to admire it. "After all, the earl has his annual festival starting tomorrow. The men – I mean, the guests will be arriving first thing in the morning. I want to look exquisite this year so I am sure to be noticed."

"Who could miss ye?" mumbled Morag under her breath.

"Willow, for a girl who says she never wants to marry, you sure do care a lot about making a lasting impression on every knight, duke or earl that visits Rothbury." Maira shook her head.

"She wants them to bed her," said Morag, handing Maira one of the lanterns.

"Nay, I don't!" Willow truly was curious about the acts of lovemaking, but she didn't want to admit it. Or at least not with Branton standing right there. Plus, if she admitted anything, it would be to Maira, and not to Morag. "After all, we see what happens when someone makes love. Morag, look at your sister. Fia is pregnant from coupling with Alastair. I will never end up with a stomach bigger than my breasts."

"Oh, I almost forgot," said Branton, holding a finger in the air. "Lord Beaufort also told me that your father will be here first thing in the morning, Willow."

Willow's head snapped around in surprise. "My father is coming to Rothbury?" This was the last thing she wanted to hear. The festival started tomorrow and would continue for an entire sennight with more titled men arriving each day. Willow had planned on meeting and dancing with as many men as she could during that time, receiving as many gifts from them as possible. If her father were here, he wouldn't let her attend the festival let alone leave her chamber. "I don't want him here," she said defiantly.

"Why not?" asked Maira. "Is it because he won't approve of the way you dress? Or don't you want him seeing you flirting with all the men?"

"Mayhap, he's comin' to Rothbury to send ye to a convent like he threatened to do as soon as ye started noticin' the laddies." Morag sounded as if she were trying to hold back a laugh.

"Enough!" spat Willow. "Let's get back to the castle. The wind is picking up, and I'm cold." She clutched her cloak to her neck, trying to close out the late October chill.

"No' yet. We need to pay our respects to Imanie before we leave." Morag headed over to the gravesite.

"Nay, we don't." Willow no longer wanted to stay in the garden now that she had what she had come for. "You only said that because you are feeling guilty again for being the one to kill her, aren't you, Morag?"

"I didna kill her." Morag looked up with tears in her eyes. Her hand shot up and covered the heart brooch she wore that symbolized she was one of the Followers of the Secret Heart. She wasn't chosen by the late queen and therefore had no right to be a member. It was Imanie who gave her the brooch right off her own bodice and let her join the order. However, the old woman had mentioned that the last time she brought someone into the group, there was a death. If she brought anyone into the secret group that was not invited by the queen, this could happen again. It did. Imanie gave Morag the brooch, and then she died.

"Let's stop at the grave and quickly pay our respects," suggested Maira. "After all, Imanie was our mentor. We owe her that."

"If Fia were here, she'd make us all get down on our knees and say a prayer for Imanie," Morag announced.

"I'm not kneeling on the ground in this gown, and neither am I staying out in the cold any longer than I have to," retorted Willow. "If we're going to pay our respects then let's do it and be on our way."

The three girls stood with Branton, holding out their lanterns and looking down at the grave of Imanie. Willow's eyes and mouth dropped open when she thought she saw a shadow pass over the grave. She spun around to look behind her, but there was no one there.

"That's enough. Let's go," she said, hurrying for her horse, anxious to leave. There was a presence here, and she wasn't sure if it was an intruder or perhaps a ghost. Or, mayhap, it was only her imagination. Either way, it didn't matter. All she wanted was to get back to the castle because she felt as if someone were watching them.

CHAPTER 2

"Willow, wake up!" Maira shook Willow by the shoulders. "Your father is already here, and he says he has some exciting news."

"Aye," agreed Morag. "He arrived over an hour ago and has been waitin' for ye to get out of bed before he tells us. Hurry up, I canna wait any longer."

Willow opened one sleepy eye and sat up and yawned and stretched. "Father is here?" she asked, trying to get her bearings, hoping she had heard them wrong.

"That's right, I'm here, and I'm no longer willing to wait in the great hall." Willow's father, Rook, burst into the room. Maira's father, Rowen was right behind him. The two men, along with Morag and Fia's father, Reed, were triplets and also bastards of the late King Edward III. The only way to tell the men apart was by the color of their hair. Rook had hair like a midnight sky. Rowen was blond like the shining sun. And Reed had bright red hair like fire.

"Father! Uncle Rowen!" Willow pulled the blanket up to her chin to hide her night-rail. "What are you doing here? I am not even out of bed yet, and certainly not dressed."

"I can see that, and it disgusts me that you have become so lazy, Willow." Rook marched over to the shutter and pulled it open, letting in the sunlight as well as a cold breeze. "Your mother is not going to like it when I tell her that our only daughter has been acting as if she thinks she's a queen."

"Father, close the shutter," complained Willow, sinking down into the covers. "It's cold in here."

"What's the news?" asked Morag anxiously. "Tell us, Uncle Rook, please. I canna wait any longer."

"It's about your sister," Rowen spoke for him.

"What do ye mean? What about Fia?" Morag clutched the bedpost, and her eyes opened wide. "She isna ill, is she?"

"Nay," said Rook with a shake of his head. "She –"

"She's had her baby," Rowen interrupted before Rook could tell them.

"I was getting to that," growled Rook, throwing his brother a daggered look.

"She has a bairn!" Morag excitedly jumped up and down. Once again, as far as Willow was concerned, Morag was acting childish.

"Was it a boy or a girl?" asked Maira.

"A girl," answered Rowen. "They named her Oletha after Alastair's mother. Reed is boasting that he has not

11

only the first grandchild but also the most girls in the family."

"Aye. We'll never hear the end of it," agreed Rook. "Thank goodness he doesn't have the most boys, or there'd be no living with him at all."

"I am so excited," said Morag. "I canna wait to see Fia and the baby. Can we leave right away?"

"That's why we're here," said Rowen. "We're going to escort you three to the Highlands, leaving today. Fia requested that you three be there to help her celebrate."

"We're leaving today?" Willow sat up straighter in bed. "But can't it wait until after the Autumn Harvest Festival?"

"Nay, Willow. That will last a sennight," said Maira. "Fia is waiting for us now, and we need to be there for her."

"I suppose you're right," Willow answered with a sigh. She wanted to be with her cousin but also longed to stay here for the festival.

"I willna wait another day," said Morag. "Come on, Willow, get out of bed so we can leave."

"Give me some time." Willow didn't want to get out from under the covers with the men in the room.

Rowen looked out the window and whistled lowly.

"What is it?" asked Maira.

"It looks like a caravan of knights coming across the drawbridge," Rowen told them. "Beaufort must have invited a lot of nobles to his festival."

"Knights?" Willow's ears perked up.

"I want to see," said Morag running to the window.

"I suppose I should get up." Willow pulled the blanket

off the bed, wrapping it around her. She padded across the floor in bare feet to see the procession of men entering the courtyard. The herald blew the straight trumpet and started to announce the men one by one.

"The Lord and Lady Pellington of Dover," he said, blowing the horn in between each name he announced. "Earl Roger Herrington of Devon. Lord and Lady Simon Boshce of Northumbria. Sir Carl de Verre of Suffolk."

Willow pushed her way between her cousins to see out the window. One after another, the nobles piled into the courtyard. Squires held poles fluttering with the crests of the knights as the horses whickered and clomped across the cobbled stones. It was a grand procession, and even the horses wore decorated bridles and saddles and long coverings depicting each of the knights' crests. Lord Beaufort and Lady Ernestine sat atop a wooden dais, greeting each knight, baron, and earl with a nod of their heads.

Willow's heart raced in excitement. The noble entourage held her interest. She had never seen anything as impressive in her life, except for when she visited her cousin, King Richard, at court once a year. Each year the festival became better and better.

"There's quite a crowd," said Rook, walking up behind Willow and laying his hands on her shoulders. "Look, there is Sir Bedivere of Gaunt."

Rowen moaned. "I wonder why Beaufort invited him."

"Probably because he's one of the richest knights in all of England," answered Rook.

"He's also the greediest," said Rowen.

"Sir Bedivere is handsome." Willow stretched her neck, perusing the tall man with dark, trimmed hair and mustache.

"You stay away from him. He's a womanizer," warned Rook, his large hands gripping Willow's shoulders tighter.

"Aye, he's ruined more than a dozen ladies that I know of, and most likely another dozen servant girls," agreed Rowen.

"Father, I'm not a child anymore," said Willow with a sigh and a roll of her eyes. "I don't need you telling me to stay away from men. Besides, I am already well past marrying age and might want to choose a husband someday."

"You'll choose no one. I'll decide who you marry and when," Rook warned her. "You are not ready to take a husband yet."

"Grandfather told me on his deathbed that I can choose my own husband."

"He said you could agree or disagree, but I will be the one who gives you the choice of which man to marry."

Willow didn't want to argue with her father, so she said nothing more.

"Look over there." Rowen pointed out the window as another man rode into the courtyard. "Isn't that the page boy you mentored years ago, Rook? You remember, the one that you really admired?"

"Let me see." Rook released Willow and stepped closer to the window. "Aye, it is, indeed. Sir Conrad," he called out the window, waving his arm, trying to get the man's attention. "Sir Conrad, up here."

"Father, it's not proper to be shouting and waving your arm out the window! What will people think?" Willow stepped back, embarrassed by her father's actions.

"Neither was it proper to live in the catacombs, but yet it didn't bother me at all to do it," said Rook. "Then again, I'm a man. It doesn't matter. You just worry about what is proper for a lady."

"Aye, Father," she answered, not knowing why the same rules didn't apply to men and women both.

"Look, Willow, it's Sir Conrad Lochwood," her father told her, motioning with his head out to the courtyard.

"Who?" she asked, pretending not to recognize the name of the boy who grew up as her father's ward.

"It's Conrad," he said. "You used to play with him when you were little, before coming to Rothbury to be mentored. I'm sure you remember him."

Aye, she remembered Conrad all right. But she was far from excited about seeing him again. "Father, Conrad used to pull my braids and hide frogs in my bed," she told him, wrinkling her nose as she said it. "Why on earth would I want to see Conrad the Cur? I despise him." She didn't bother to look out the window.

"Willow, you are being haughty again," Rook scolded her. "Conrad was just a boy when he did those things. You haven't seen him since you've been living here in Rothbury. He's a grown man and a knight now."

"I don't care." Willow yawned and stretched one arm

out from under the blanket she held around her. "I still don't like him."

"Daughter, how many times do I have to tell you to cover your mouth when you yawn?" asked her father.

"I do cover it," she told him. "But I'm only around family, so what does it matter?" She scratched the back of her head next.

"And stop itching yourself like a flea-ridden scullery maid," snapped Rook. "Now hurry and get dressed, because we need to take to the road right away."

The herald called out another name next that interested Willow very much.

"Earl Stanley Alnwick," he announced.

Upon hearing this, Willow shot over to the window, almost knocking over Maira who was leaning her elbows on the ledge.

"What's the hurry?" asked Maira, scowling at her. "Be careful."

"That's him," said Willow, feeling the rise of a flush to her cheeks. "He's the one with the ruby as big as his hand that he's bringing as a gift to the king. He's stopping here to show it to the earl. I can't wait to see it. Mayhap he'll let me hold it as well."

"Ye like him because he's rich, dinna ye?" asked Morag.

"She likes all the men if you haven't noticed." Maira left the window and headed across the room.

"Don't be silly! Earl Alnwick is old, not to mention married. And I do not like all of the men," said Willow, thinking about Sir Conrad. How she'd like to give him a piece of her mind for putting sugar in the salt cellar and convincing her to put lots of it on her fish on her eighth birthday. After taking one bite and almost gagging, she threw the trencher at Conrad. Because of it, she was punished by her father for a sennight. Of course, she told Rook that it was Conrad who started it, but Rook seemed to favor the boy. Instead, her father told her she was not acting like a lady.

"Willow, we are leaving within the hour," Rook told her from the door. "We won't be back for a sennight, so be sure to have your handmaid pack everything you will need for the visit."

"A sennight?" asked Willow, realizing that by the time they returned, the festival would be over. She will have missed it all. "Why so long?"

"Dinna be daft, Willow." Morag crossed her arms over her chest and rolled her eyes. "Ye ken it takes longer to get to the Highlands where Fia now lives."

"And Fia will want us to stay and visit with her since we've only seen her twice in the past year," added Maira. "I wouldn't mind staying longer if we have the chance."

"I'll tell Lord Beaufort our stay might be extended," said Rook.

"Extended?" Willow glanced back out the window at the noble procession, feeling her heart drop. She had been looking forward to this for so long. Now because Fia had birthed her baby, Willow was going to miss it all.

Willow wanted more than anything to go with them to be with her cousin and to see her new niece. But then again, this festival only came once a year. Willow secretly hoped to find a man that interested her that she could possibly marry in the future. She didn't want to tell her cousins this, but since there were so many nobles in one place, it would make her options more viable. "Father, I think I am feeling ill," said Willow, clutching her stomach and heading back to the bed.

"What?" Rook looked up and frowned. "I'll call for the healer, anon."

Her head snapped up. "Nay! I'm sure it's nothing that requires a healer."

"Really?" He furrowed his brow. "Then what is it?"

"It's . . . it's . . ." What could she possibly say to get her father to leave her behind? It wasn't likely he was going to agree to it, so she had to sound convincing. There was only one thing she could tell him that would work. "It's my menses," she whispered, watching her father's reaction. He stood up and cleared his throat and looked the other way. "I can't possibly ride a horse up to the Highlands now. I think I'd better stay behind." She let out a sigh to add some drama to the situation. "I am so going to miss seeing Fia and the baby. Do give her my regards."

"If you can't ride, then we'll take a wagon," said Rook. "I wouldn't want you to miss out on seeing the baby."

Willow felt so frustrated that she wanted to scream. She looked over to her cousins with pleading eyes. Morag would never help her but perhaps Maira would. "Traveling over the bumpy ground is going to upset the way I feel."

She nodded slightly to Maira, hoping she'd understand that she was looking for a backup.

Maira shook her head and made a face. "Aye, Uncle Rook, that's right," she said, not at all sounding convincing. "Willow will feel terrible and ruin the trip for all of us if she comes along. Plus, she will only slow us down. I think she should stay here."

"Willow, I don't like the idea of leaving you behind." Rook frowned, his dark eyebrows angling downward.

"Especially with the festival going on," added Rowen, throwing his brother a look that Willow was sure meant that they thought she was faking it.

"Please, Father?" she asked, giving him the little pout that she had used through the years that always made her father give in to her wishes.

"Willow, don't do that," said Rook, looking like he was about to surrender.

"I won't be any trouble staying here in Rothbury if that's what you're worried about."

"I don't know that this is a good idea."

"I'll be no trouble to Lord Beaufort at all. I would really like to stay in Rothbury for the festival, Father."

Rook ran a hand through his long, dark hair, looking in the opposite direction.

"Please?" she asked in the sweetest voice she could muster up.

Her father released an exasperated sigh and threw his hands in the air. "Fine, stay here, then."

"Oh, thank you, Father." Willow ran over and hugged her father, nearly dropping the blanket in the process.

"But," he added, raising a finger in the air. Willow slowly released him.

"But?" she asked, looking up with wide eyes.

"I'm going to hire Sir Conrad to watch over you while I'm gone."

Willow's mouth dropped open. "Sir Conrad? Nay! I don't want him anywhere near me."

"And that's exactly why I'm asking him and not one of the other nobles that will be attending the festival. If you are staying behind with all these men arriving, Sir Conrad will watch you like a hawk, young lady."

"But Father –"

"Don't give me the pout again, Willow because it won't work. I know you too well, and you can't fool me. You want to stay here because of the noblemen that are arriving. If I force you to come with us, you'll only make our trip a living hell. So, stay here where you'll be happy."

"But I won't be happy with Conrad looking over my shoulder and watching my every move." A shudder ran through her body at the thought of it. She pictured his greasy, unkempt hair, his scrawny, lanky body, and the bumpy skin. From what she remembered, he was a homely boy.

"It's either that or you get dressed and come with us. What's your decision?" Rook crossed his arms over his chest and waited for her answer.

Willow felt doomed. This was going to ruin all her

plans. But she had no choice other than to accept the offer. Perhaps, she could manage to lose Conrad who would be shadowing her during the festival. Then she would still be able to enjoy the festivities after all. "Fine. Conrad the Cur it is, then."

"Willow," he said in a warning voice. "Do not call him names. You will respect him and listen to every word he says. Do you understand?"

"What? Nay, Father." She shook her head, trying to make the awful thought leave her mind.

"He's a knight now, and any squabbles you've had in the past with him will be buried and left in the past."

She didn't answer but instead looked at the ground.

"Willow? Do you understand me?"

"I do, Father," she finally said in defeat, knowing this is the only way she'd be able to stay and attend the festival.

"And I will make sure to tell Sir Conrad that if you behave improperly around the men, that he is to take you immediately to Whitby Abbey and leave you there until I return to collect you."

"I told ye that ye'd end up in an abbey." Morag had a smile on her face that only made Willow more irritated.

"Can we go now?" asked Maira impatiently, checking her weapons that she always wore.

"Aye," said Rook with a nod of his head. "Now come here and give me a goodbye hug, Daughter."

Willow's eyes darted from one person to the other in the room. "Father, please stop. You are embarrassing me."

"I don't hug you around others . . . only around family,"

said Rook with a smile that told her that two could play her game.

"Thank you for letting me stay," said Willow, hugging her father, dreading the thought that for the next week she'd be followed around by Sir Conrad – a man she truly despised.

CHAPTER 3

"*P*ardon me, Sir Rook, but you'd like me to do what?" asked Sir Conrad Lochwood, taking a tankard of ale from a serving wench in the great hall. He'd arrived here not a half-hour ago with his squire and sister, and was surprised to see the man who had mentored him and been his guardian. He was also surprised to know Rook wanted him to watch over his unruly, stuffy daughter. Memories of the girl were still embedded in his mind, and they were all unpleasant.

"I'm more than willing to pay you whatever you'll require to see this through," said Rook.

"I'm here for the festival," explained Conrad. He took a swig of ale, cooling his parched throat. His eyes scanned the room, settling on his younger sister who waited by the entrance of the great hall with his squire, Toby. He had enough worries just trying to watch over her now that his mother had died. "I don't think I'll be able to take you up on your offer, but thank you just the same."

"Conrad," said Rook, throwing his arm over Conrad's shoulder, almost making him spill his ale. "Tell me; how are you doing? When you were knighted three years ago, you left, and I haven't heard from you since."

"I've been busy caring for my ailing mother after my father passed away last year."

"So sorry to hear about your father. And how is your mother faring?" asked Rook.

"She's dead. Died two days ago."

"Oh, I had no idea." Rook removed his arm from around Conrad's shoulder. "You had a younger sister, too, if I'm not mistaken. What was her name? Hattie?"

"Hazel," he said. "She is four and ten years of age, and is now in my care."

"Ah, I suppose she's waiting for you back at your manor house."

"Nay. She was too distraught at the death of our mother. I had no choice but to bring her with me. She's right there." He nodded to Hazel, who looked up with frightened eyes.

"You brought her with you?" asked Rook in confusion.

"She's very shaken and scared and trusts no one. I couldn't leave her alone," replied Conrad. "To be honest, I brought her here hoping that the earl would let her be his ward now, the way he is for your daughter and nieces. However, he told me he has no time or patience to be guardian to one more young woman."

"That's a shame," said Rook, putting his hand to his chin in thought. "But I think I know how I can help you."

"How so?" asked Conrad.

"Ever since Willow moved here to be fostered by the earl at the late queen's command, my wife has really missed having a daughter around the castle. I'm sure I could find room to take in Hazel for a few years and mentor her for you. My wife would care for her as if she were the girl's own mother."

"That would be wonderful," said Conrad, knowing his sister would be in good hands. The thought relieved him. Hazel needed special care that Conrad couldn't give her. He had the utmost respect for Sir Rook. "That will give me time to get things in order back at the manor house. I had hoped to find a suitable wife and then bring Hazel to live with us, but I just haven't had the time. I thank you very much."

"Of course," said Rook. He paused for a moment and then looked up from his ale. "But it'll have to wait for a sennight since I am on my way to the Highlands with my nieces to see my brother, Reed's new grandchild."

"That's fine," said Conrad. "I don't mind waiting." He took another drink of ale from his tankard.

"You can wait right here at Castle Rothbury since the festivities will be going on for that long anyway."

"I suppose I could if the baron would have me as his guest the entire time. I wouldn't want my sister to have to sleep in a tent outside the castle walls like the rest of the visitors."

"Did you want me to put in a good word for you?" Rook looked up and smiled. Suddenly, Conrad felt as if he'd been had.

"I know that look," said Conrad. "You're about to make me some kind of deal that I won't be able to turn down."

"You know me too well, Sir Conrad. I figure since you'll be here waiting for me anyway, you can take me up on my offer to watch over Willow until my return."

Conrad groaned inwardly. Rook had him over a barrel. How could he turn him down when Rook just offered to be his sister's guardian? It would solve a lot of problems for Conrad and take the weight off his shoulders. He had no choice but to accept the deal.

"You only want me to keep an eye on Willow, and that's it?" he asked, making sure he understood what would be required of him.

"Aye. I want you to watch her and keep every man here away from her."

"What? Wait." Conrad felt doomed. "I'm sorry, but I've heard of your daughter's reputation. Keeping her away from the men would be like trying to keep a fish alive out of water."

Rook's jaw clenched, and the corner of his mouth twitched. "What have you heard about my daughter? And what do you mean by *her reputation?*"

Conrad regretted speaking so freely now. The last thing he wanted to do was anger Rook. He should have chosen his words more carefully. "I – just meant that I've heard she is a beautiful young lady now and all the men are vying for her attention." He hadn't really heard that at all. The gossip was that Willow was naught but a flirt and no man seriously looking for a wife would ever consider marrying her. Still, Rook didn't need to hear that about his only daughter. It would only make him furious. He'd want to kill any man who said it aloud.

Rook's frown turned into a smile, making Conrad realize he had managed to mend the situation.

"Aye, she is quite a beauty. That is what worries me," said Rook. "I don't trust any man around her. I am sure they will all be after her virtue."

"I'm sure," said Conrad, thinking this was going to be a long week. "I will do my best to keep her away from the men. I mean, I will keep the men away from her, my lord."

"Good. Then we have a deal. How much do you want?"

Conrad glanced back at his sister who was motioning for him to join her. It looked like she felt uncomfortable standing there. She had a hard time just talking to his squire since she was a very timid girl. He didn't know how to help her overcome her shyness as well as her fears. The sooner she was taken into Rook's care the better. The girl really needed a mother to raise her, not a brother.

"Oh, I couldn't take money from you." Conrad waved a hand through the air in a dismissing manner. "Not when you are going to mentor Hazel upon your return."

"Have it your way." Rook finished off his ale.

"Hazel needs to be around another woman at her age,

and I'm afraid there are things a brother cannot teach her. The sooner your wife takes her under her wing the better. The past few years my mother had been too ill to be of any help with Hazel. So please hurry back, my lord." He lifted his tankard to his mouth and started to drink.

"Hazel can stay with Willow until my return," said Rook.

Conrad almost choked on his ale. "With Willow? Nay, that's not necessary, my lord." Visions of his sister in a low-cut bodice and three men clinging to her arm flitted through his head. Willow was not at all who he wanted mentoring his little sister.

"Of course," said Rook. "Willow would be happy to have her. My brother and I are taking her cousins to the Highlands, so I am sure she will be anxious for the company of another girl until her cousins return."

"We're ready, Uncle Rook." Two girls walked up with Rook's brother, Rowen.

"Hello, Sir Conrad," said Rowen. "You've grown much taller since the last time I saw you." He reached out and pumped Conrad's hand.

"Sir Conrad will be watching over Willow while we're gone, so we are free to leave now," Rook explained.

"You're going to be watching over my cousin?" asked the girl with the sword strapped to her back.

"Sir Conrad, I'd like you to meet my daughter, Maira," said Rowen.

"And I'm her cousin, Morag," said the other girl.

Conrad thought the girls were attractive and became curious as to what Willow looked like now.

"Sir Conrad, my daughter's chamber is at the top of the stairs and down at the end of the corridor," Rook told him. "Please tell her our arrangements. If she has any questions, have her meet me in the stable within the next ten minutes. If not, I'll be gone."

With that, Rook, Rowen, and the girls headed away.

"My lord," said Conrad's squire, Toby, heading over with Hazel right behind him. "My lord, Lady Hazel doesn't feel comfortable standing in the great hall, not knowing anyone."

"Then introduce her to some people." Conrad shoved his empty tankard into Toby's hand. "Now, if you'll all excuse me, I have an errand to run that I am not anticipating is going to go smoothly at all."

* * *

WILLOW TIED the front laces of her bodice as she kept her eyes fastened out the open window. The guests were arriving quickly. She had to hurry and get down to the courtyard to meet the men. If she moved faster, she might get first pick amongst the unmarried lords and knights. Without her sister and cousins here, there shouldn't be much competition at all.

"My crown," she said, hurrying over and picking up the jeweled crown on her dressing table, placing it on her head. The late queen had willed crowns to her, Fia, and

Maira, as well as heart brooches that depicted them to be members of the secret society of strong women called the Followers of the Secret Heart.

She reached out and picked up her brooch, running a loving hand over it as thoughts of Imanie filled her head. The old woman told them they all had unique skills. Fia's talent was the power of observation and reading body language. Maira's skill was her ability to handle weapons.

"What about me?" Willow asked Imanie. "I don't like to fight, like Maira. What is my strength?"

"She only likes to dress up and bat her eyes at men," Morag told her, making the rest of the girls laugh.

"Don't laugh," scolded Imanie. "Even that can be a strength as well."

"It can?" asked Willow. "How?"

"It is by the persuasiveness of many strong women in the past that the queen was able to find out secrets that helped the king and his army to be successful."

"Persuasive? With enemies?" asked Willow's cousin, Fia.

"Yes, with enemies as well as with friends. Men always seem to hold secrets within them. It is our job as Followers of the Secret Heart to draw those secrets from them to use to our advantage. Willow, you have a special way with words."

Willow smiled as she pinned the heart on her bodice. She wanted to do something special and important, like Fia. She might not be able to stop a war, but Willow was sure if the time came, she would be able to use her particular skill with people to help her country or someone important in some way. She wished she knew if there were other members of the secret group out there somewhere. If so, she would like to meet them.

Fia had found a member named Lorraine. But now Lorraine was dead. If only they had been able to get more information from her, then possibly they would know where to go to find others who wore the same heart brooch.

A knock on the door dragged her from her thoughts. She figured it was her handmaid, and called out over her shoulder.

"Enter."

Picking up Imanie's ring, she slipped it on her finger and then put the bracelet on her wrist as well.

"Lady Willow?" asked a deep voice from behind her.

Willow spun on her heel, her heart racing at hearing a man's voice in her room. There in the doorway stood a tall, handsome knight. He gripped the edge of the doorframe with one hand but stayed outside the room. Unless it was her imagination, he was hesitant to enter.

"Aye," she said, her voice squeaking since she was so mesmerized by the man's appearance. Hopefully, he was one of the unmarried knights here for the festival. She would like to get to know him. "I am Willow. Lady Willow Douglas." She reached up and straightened the crown on her head.

"Your father sent me."

"My father?" She cocked her head, taking two steps toward the man. He looked familiar. Where had she seen his face before? "Who are you, Sir Knight? And why has my father sent you to my door?"

"Willow, it's me. Conrad," said the man with a comforting smile.

"Conrad?" Her mouth fell open, and she blinked twice, thinking this was all a dream. "Conrad . . . who?" she asked, just to make sure. After all, this couldn't possibly be the same lanky boy with the bad skin and the greasy hair that she remembered from childhood. Nay. This man had a broad chest and many muscles in his arms. Shiny oaken hair came to the nape of his neck. And his skin was impeccably smooth like the sand on the beach after a wave washed back out to the sea.

"Sir Conrad Lochwood." He cleared his throat and shifted from one foot to the other. "I thought you'd remember me from my time being mentored by your father at Naward Castle. Of course, that was a long time ago."

So it was him! God had been kind to the man after all. She would never have dreamed in a million years that Conrad the Cur would be standing in her doorway looking like a handsome man.

"I – I am sorry. It's been a long time, and I didn't recognize you." She smoothed out her gown and sashayed toward him. "Won't you come in and close the door?"

Almost as if she'd struck him, the man jumped backward, nearly falling over his feet. "Nay," he said backing out into the corridor. "It wouldn't be proper. Your father wouldn't like it."

"My father told me just today that it doesn't matter if a man acts properly or not. He won't care if you come into my chamber. Besides, you told me yourself that he sent you here, so it's all right to enter." She moved closer.

"I am here only to tell you that –"

"Stop," she said, holding up her hand. "I don't think whatever the message is, that you should be saying it out in the corridor where the servants are listening to every word." She nodded to a chambermaid passing by, and a page walking the other way. They both moved slowly, and it was apparent they wondered why he was there. So did Willow, although she could guess. The reason was one she thought she'd hate, but now she wasn't so certain. "At least step into the room and close the door partially, because I don't want you announcing my father's business to the entire castle."

"Oh, I suppose you are right." He looked over his shoulder and then stepped into the room, closing the door part way behind him.

As handsome as he was, he was still the boy who had yanked her braids, played practical tricks on her, and made her life a living hell before she was sent to be fostered by Lord Beaufort. Her father sent her away from Naward because it was what the late queen wanted. In doing so, he took her away from her mother as well. Willow missed her mother and was only glad she lived with her cousins because it made it easier. They comforted each other often.

"Your father has sent me here because I am to tell you that I will be your guardian until his return."

"I don't need a guardian." She put her hand out and gave the door a shove. It closed with a loud click behind him. "Now, Sir Conrad, tell me how much my father is paying you to do this. Because however much it is, I will pay you twice as much to leave Rothbury now and never look back again."

CHAPTER 4

"I'm sorry, my lord, but I'll be leaving Rothbury anon and won't be able to look after Willow after all." Conrad stood in the stable telling Lord Rook, not at all sure why he decided to leave after he'd already accepted the man's offer. Willow was the one who convinced him to do it. He'd never seen anything like it before. She had an uncanny power of persuasion. Before he knew what happened, she'd gotten him to agree to leave and proceeded to push him out the door.

"She paid you to leave, didn't she?" asked Rook, peering down at Conrad from atop his horse. He frowned and his eyes narrowed. "How much did she give you?" Rook picked up his pouch and shook the coins inside. Rowen and Willow's cousins were on the other side of the stable and looked up when they heard the jingling. "I'll give you more. Price is no object. Just tell me how much you want."

"Nay, my lord, you don't understand," said Conrad,

raising his hands in the air. He felt as if he were caught in the middle of a challenging situation.

"Here. Take the whole damned bag of coins; I don't care. Just please don't leave her side until I return." Rook tossed the bag to Conrad who instinctively caught it.

"Father, I came to say goodbye." Willow's singsong voice came from the door. Conrad spun on his heel to see her entering the stable. His squire and sister entered right behind her. "What are you doing?" she asked, making him feel like a scolded child. Her tone and the way she scowled at him made him feel as if he'd been caught doing something wrong. He followed her gaze down to his hands only to realize, to his horror, he held Rook's pouch of coins, and it didn't look good. "Why are you still here and what is that?" With a snap of her wrist, she pointed at the pouch.

"Lady Willow." Conrad swallowed the lump in his throat. He couldn't get over how pretty she was, even when she was angry. Even in childhood, Willow had been adorable. Her heart-shaped face was graced with the biggest, round, brown eyes he'd ever seen in his life. Everything about her was very feminine and perfect, from the way she stood and walked to the tilt of her chin that she raised ever so slightly in an intimidating manner.

"My father paid you to stay, didn't he?" Willow's eyes narrowed, just like her father's.

"Nay, I didn't take the money, although he offered." Conrad reached out to hand the pouch back to Rook.

"I'll not be outbid by my own daughter," spat Rook. "Take the money, Lochwood. We had a deal."

"You were supposed to be leaving," said Willow, putting her hands on her hips.

"I can't believe you let a woman outbid me," came Rook's reply.

"Stop it! All of you," shouted Conrad. "I didn't take money from either of you."

"Conrad, what's going on?" asked Hazel in a small voice from across the stable.

"Aye," said Toby, glancing around the area. "Are we leaving or staying? I'm confused."

Conrad looked first at Willow's glaring eyes, and next his gaze traveled over to his sister. She seemed so frightened and insecure. Hazel's grey eyes studied him anxiously. She needed guidance that he couldn't give her. Then he looked over at Lord Rook who stared down at him from atop his horse. Conrad still held the bag of coins in his hand. He didn't want the money. What he wanted was Lord Rook to be Hazel's guardian. Rook's wife, Calliope, was supposedly a kind-hearted woman who never turned away anyone in need. Yes, she could take his sister under her wing while Conrad looked for a wife and saw to things back in Scarborough.

"What'll it be, Lochwood?" asked Rowen, leading his horse over to join them. Willow's cousins were already mounted on their horses and headed over as well.

"Lochwood is staying in Rothbury to watch over Willow until my return," announced Rook.

"Nay, Father. I will not have him dogging my heels everywhere I go," complained Willow.

"You could always come with us to see Fia's baby," suggested Maira.

"Aye, my sister did request ye to come to the Highlands as well," added Morag.

Conrad could see by the look on Willow's face that she struggled with her decision. But if she went with them, the deal Lord Rook made with Conrad of being Hazel's guardian would probably fall through. Hazel needed lots of care and attention. She had problems that Conrad didn't know how to fix. That would take away from Conrad's plan to find a wife to bring back to Scarborough. Nay, he couldn't let Willow go to the Highlands with them. This was an opportunity he had to take.

"I'll stay here with Willow, but I won't take your money." Conrad reached up and gave the pouch of coins back to Rook.

"Good," said Rook, hooking the pouch at his side. "Willow, you will listen to Sir Conrad, and I don't want to hear that you gave him any trouble while I was gone."

"Father! How could you?" asked Willow in a huff.

"Come, girls, we have a long trip ahead of us." Rook led the way with Rowen, Maira, and Morag following right behind him.

As soon as they left, Conrad turned to Willow. "Lady Willow, I would like you to meet my sister, Hazel."

"Hello," said Hazel, shyly, looking up with her eyes but not lifting her head.

"You're his sister?" Willow looked at Conrad from the corners of her eyes.

"Your father said that Hazel will be sharing your chamber with you." Conrad watched as Willow's jaw tightened.

"My bedchamber? I'm to share my bedchamber with her?"

"Aye, it will be nice for both of you," agreed Toby.

"I don't share my bedchamber with anyone."

"Really." It was only one word, but as soon as Conrad said it, he wished he could take it back. Willow's eyes lit up with fire.

"Sir Lochwood, I advise you to keep your comments to yourself while at Rothbury," Willow warned him. "And I also advise you to stay out of my way, or you will be sorry."

She turned away in a huff and stormed from the stable.

"She doesn't seem to like me," said Hazel, lowering her eyes and looking at the ground. Conrad felt angry at Willow for the way she had acted. His sister needed a boost in confidence, not someone to make her feel worse.

"I don't believe that's the case at all," said Conrad, watching Willow sweep across the courtyard, stopping to chat with several lords and knights along the way. She smiled and giggled and seemed like an entirely different person now. There was no sign of the angry girl who had left his side just moments ago. Willow could turn her emotions on and off at the drop of a gauntlet. Very interesting, indeed.

"My lord, she did seem cold to Hazel," Toby pointed out.

"It's me that she doesn't like," Conrad explained,

holding on to the stable gate, still staring out the door. Willow flitted from one man to the next like a butterfly testing the nectar of each flower. To him, she was cold and cruel, but to these total strangers, she held all the warmth of the sun. "She doesn't like me," he repeated. "But I intend on changing all that very soon."

* * *

"EARL ALNWICK, is it true you are transporting a ruby the size of your palm to King Richard's court?" Willow had managed to avoid Conrad during the meal, as well as his sister, Hazel. She wore her crown, one of her best gowns, and Imanie's jewelry. Having stayed at her guardian's side all evening, the earl, Lord Walter Beaufort, introduced her to all the nobles at the celebration. One by one, Willow had the chance to meet the earls, barons, knights, and lords. There were no other women besides the earl's wife included, so she got all the attention. Willow always loved being the center of attention, and especially when handsome men were involved.

"My dear, that isn't a proper thing to ask the earl," Walter's wife, Ernestine, scolded Willow.

True, Willow had pushed her luck asking such a question, but she had to know for sure. She had never seen a gemstone that large and wanted not only to see it, but also to hold it in her hand.

"Why, yes, it's true," said Earl Alnwick, his facial expression telling her that he was surprised she knew. "I am transporting a ruby, but I'm afraid to say it is more the size of my thumbnail than my palm," chuckled Alnwick.

"Earl Alnwick, perhaps it isn't a good idea to speak of the stone with so many ears listening," warned Beaufort.

"I suppose you're right," answered Alnwick.

Willow didn't want the conversation to end this way and had to do something fast to change Earl Alnwick's mind, or she would never have a chance to lay her eyes on the gemstone.

"Oh, I'm certain Earl Alnwick has already considered this and has the gemstone well-guarded. Don't you, Earl Alnwick?" Willow purposely used the man's name twice and would use it a few more times before her conversation was finished. By complimenting the man and having him hear his name springing from the lips of a young, attractive girl, she was sure she could convince him to show it to her after all. "You are known to have the best guards in all of England and the most expensive and ornate secure chests in which you keep your jewels. Earl Alnwick, I am amazed that my cousin, King Richard, hasn't asked you to join his court as one of his advisors by now. I am sure there is a lot you could teach him."

Lord Beaufort let out a sigh and shook his head. "Lady Willow, I'm sure the earl doesn't have time for small talk and would like to be seen to his chamber since he has been traveling today." He raised his hand and snapped his fingers, calling over one of his pages. "Please escort the earl to his solar in the east wing."

"Aye, my lord," answered the boy.

"I had hoped to see the ruby and learn more about it," Willow continued in one last attempt. "After all – Earl Alnwick – I only wanted to compliment my cousin, the king, on the expensive present you are bringing him. I will tell him myself that you would fit in nicely not just at court but also close to his side."

"Really?" The earl perked up at hearing that, and his spine straightened. He stood a little taller.

"Lady Willow, that's enough," warned Beaufort, having learned of her power to persuade. After being in his care for nearly ten years, he grew wise to her ways. But even knowing what she was capable of doing, he still fell prey to her persuasion as well. It was because of her that she and her cousins were able to keep leaving the castle unescorted to meet in the queen's secret garden.

"What's this about a ruby?" Two men walked up to join them, having overheard the conversation. One was tall and very thin and the other short and stocky. Willow realized many people probably heard them. The room was so crowded with everyone coming for the festival that they were all bumping elbows.

"Lady Willow, have you met the Barons George of Canterbury and Chester of Ashington?" asked Beaufort.

"It's my pleasure to meet you," said Willow extending her arm. First, the stockier man, Chester, kissed her hand and then the tall one, George. They were both handsome and were sure to have land and money since they were barons.

"And I'm Sir Bedivere of Gaunt, my lady."

Willow turned to find the dark-haired knight staring into her eyes. His gaze was mesmerizing. For a moment, she almost lost herself in his dark orbs. He had a mustache and partial beard that was neatly trimmed. He looked to be only a few years older than her. He bowed and took hold of her hand and kissed it – letting the kiss linger. Her heart fluttered. So many handsome men who were all nobles. She enjoyed every minute of it but needed to know if they were married.

"I'm pleased to meet all of you." Willow nodded. "I would love to be introduced to your wives as well. Or didn't you bring them along?" Willow scanned the room quickly and waited for their answers.

"Oh, nay, we're not married," said George, speaking for him and Chester.

"Neither am I," said Bedivere, flashing her an enticing smile. "But I hope to change that soon."

"My wife stayed back at Alnwick Castle," the earl told her. "She insisted I could guard the ruby better if I didn't have to watch over her, too."

"Speaking of that . . ." To Willow's dismay, Conrad pushed his way through the men, standing close to her.

"Gentlemen, if you'll excuse Lady Willow, I need to escort her to her chamber anon."

She straightened the crown on her head that had once been the crown of the late English queen, Philippa. Alnwick's eyes roamed up to her head, and she smiled inwardly, knowing she'd caught his attention. That's when she saw him nod and press his lips together. She was sure that meant he would show her the ruby once they left the great hall.

"Earl Alnwick, my chamber is next to yours," said Willow. "Would you escort me on your way to your solar?" She smiled and tried to sound charming.

"Why, yes, I'd –"

"No need, but thank you," said Conrad, taking her by the elbow and whisking her away. Willow struggled against his hold as he all but dragged her from the great hall.

"Let go of me!" she spat, trying to pry his fingers from her arm but he would not release her. He climbed the stairs to the second floor, making sure she was in front of him. "Didn't you hear me? Release me anon."

"Not until we get to your chamber."

"I'm not going to my chamber. The dancing hasn't even begun yet."

"Dancing is out of the question unless you plan on dancing with another girl."

"A girl?" The thought appalled her. "Of course not! I'm going to dance with every man here."

"Not while I'm your guardian, you won't." He stopped outside her chamber door. "Your father instructed me to keep you away from the men until his return, and that is exactly what I'm going to do."

"He's not here, and you're not my guardian, so leave me alone, Conrad the Cur."

"Calling me names isn't going to change the situation. Now, my sister, Hazel, is already inside your chamber waiting for you, so let's hurry." He knocked quickly on the door and opened it, guiding Willow through the entrance first.

When he turned to close the door, Willow saw Earl Alnwick walk by. She nodded, giving him a coy smile.

"Stop flirting with every man here." Conrad slammed the door and stood glaring at her with his hands on his hips.

"I'm not flirting with every man, so don't make it sound as if I'm a strumpet."

"Name one man that you haven't flirted with, and I'll guarantee that you will try to do it before this festival is over."

"You," she said, smiling slightly. "I have not flirted with you and neither will I ever want to flirt with you since I despise you. So that ruins your theory." She turned away from him.

CONRAD SOMEHOW FELT slighted that she said this about him. Not wanting to flirt with him was one thing, but did she really despise him? No man wanted a beautiful woman to hate him. That only made Conrad want to try harder to get her to change her mind.

"Conrad?" came a soft voice from the other side of the room. Conrad had almost forgotten that his sister was there since she was so quiet. Willow's presence was domineering, flamboyant, and overwhelming. When she was in a room, all eyes were on her. Even Conrad had found

45

himself drawn in by not only her physical beauty but by the way she spoke and acted. It was as if each word was calculated to serve a purpose. But, at the same time, the tone of her voice made it seem effortless and spontaneous . . . and innocent. But innocent was a word that Conrad would never associate with this girl.

"Hazel." Conrad guided Willow with his hand on the small of her back as he headed toward his sister. Willow looked over her shoulder and then down his arm. Quickly, he removed his hold, feeling as if she didn't want him touching her. After all, when a woman says she despises a man, the last thing on earth she would want is for him to make contact. "Hazel, I would like you to meet Lady Willow. You will be staying with her in her chamber during the duration of our visit. I'm sure you two will enjoy each other's company."

"Humph," mumbled Willow, hurrying over to the window and throwing open the shutters. She leaned over the sill, trying to see the knights and lords in the courtyard down below. Conrad sighed and hurried after her.

"Hello," she called out, waving to someone.

"That's enough," said Conrad reaching for her just as she turned around. He must have scared her because she jerked backward and lost her balance. He grabbed her with both hands and pulled her into his arms as she almost fell out the open window. "Be careful," he said, his arms wrapping around her securely. She looked up at him and was so close that their faces almost touched. Her long, black lashes blinked more than normal, showing off her big, round, brown eyes. The girl's skin was smooth like silk, and her wavy, dark tresses cascaded loosely over her shoulders. She didn't wear her hair pulled back and tucked away beneath a wimple like a proper lady. He found himself liking the way it looked. "You could have fallen," he said, staring at her full lips. They looked so moist and soft and as if they were in need of kissing.

"I – suppose so."

When her focus shifted to his mouth, all sense left him. He became heady from the scent of lavender wafting up from her hair. She smelled fresh like a summer's day after a light rain. She had him so mesmerized that he found himself longing to know how her lips tasted. It was almost as if he'd go crazy with want if he didn't find out. Then, without thinking, he leaned over and brushed his lips gently against hers.

Excitement filled him at the contact and the taste of her sweet lips. It was like spring filled the autumn day, bringing with it a sense of rebirth.

The kiss lingered, and her head fell back as if she enjoyed it. When he pulled away, he noticed her eyes were closed.

"Conrad?" came Hazel's voice from behind him. He jerked upright and dropped his hands to his sides. Then Willow's eyes opened and just when he thought she was going to kiss him back, she slapped him instead!

"How dare you kiss me as if you had the right to?"

"Conrad?" Hazel spoke to him once again.

"Just a minute, Hazel," he said, holding up his hand, not

bothering to turn around to look at his sister. Instead, his gaze was fastened to Willow. "You wanted me to kiss you, just admit it. If not, you wouldn't have been looking at my mouth."

Willow's brows arched high in surprise. "Why, Conrad the Cur, I see some things never change. You are no different than when I first met you when I was a child!"

"What?" He didn't understand what that was supposed to mean.

"Conrad?" asked Hazel once again.

"What is it, Hazel?" He spun around with his hands in the air. His sister was at the door with a worried look on her face. In the open doorway stood not only Lord Beaufort, but also Earl Alnwick, the barons George and Chester, and Sir Bedivere. "My lords!" he said, abruptly moving away from Willow, feeling like a damned fool.

"What's going on here, Lochwood?" growled Beaufort. "Lady Willow is my ward, and I don't like what I just saw."

"What did you see?" asked Conrad, dragging a hand through his hair. His back had been to the men, and he hoped they hadn't actually seen the kiss.

"I saw Lady Willow slapping an honored and revered knight."

"Y-you did?" he asked, not sure if he saw the kiss or not. It didn't sound like it.

"Lady Willow, what do you have to say for yourself?" asked Beaufort.

"My lord." Willow stepped forward, straightening her

gown. "I had an excellent reason for slapping him. It was because he –"

"I had a mosquito on my face, and she smashed it," said Conrad, stepping forward. "Was there something that you wanted, my lords?"

"Aye," said Earl Alnwick. "Lady Willow's words made sense to me. I've decided to show all of you the ruby."

"I did that?" asked Willow, sounding surprised. "And you're going to let all of us see it?"

"He is, my dear," said Lord Beaufort. "Since you pointed out that the earl has the gem guarded securely, he decided to show the stone to some of us."

"You, too, Lochwood," said Earl Alnwick. "And I'm guessing that is the sister you spoke of, so bring her to my solar as well."

"Aye, my lord," said Conrad as the men headed down the corridor. Conrad turned back to the women. "Hazel, you'll join us," he said to his sister. Then he took Willow by the elbow and leaned over and whispered into her ear. "For a girl who calls me a cur and supposedly hates me, you sure seemed to like the kiss."

"Get away from me or I'll slap you again. And this time, the earl will know it wasn't a bug." She hurried through the door, not waiting for Conrad to escort her.

"Conrad, I tried to warn you they were here," said Hazel in her ever-so-soft, timid voice.

"Well, next time something like this happens, do me a favor and stop me from kissing her in the first place."

"Don't you like her?" Hazel looked up curiously and

waited. It was a question he didn't know how to answer. He thought he despised Willow just as much as she did him. But now she had him all confused because all he wanted to do was kiss her again, even if he received a slap in return.

"Sometimes a man gets confused and does things without even knowing why he did them."

"She doesn't seem very friendly. Lady Willow hasn't even spoken a word to me. I don't think she likes me."

"Don't take it to heart, dear sister." Conrad put his arm around Hazel's shoulders and guided her out the door. "Lady Willow doesn't seem to notice anyone unless they are a man."

CHAPTER 5

*W*illow reached out and carefully plucked the ruby from the chest that the earl's guard held out to her with two hands.

"It's beautiful," she said, reverently holding it up in the sunlight streaming in from the window. The light filtered through the red stone, being the prettiest thing she'd ever seen in her life.

"It's the sister stone of the Regale Ruby that King Louis VII of France gave to England two centuries ago," said the earl.

"How did you get it?" asked Conrad.

"Where do we find more of these?" asked Sir George with a chuckle.

"My grandfather made a shrewd deal years ago and passed it down to me," said the earl.

"Why are you giving it to the king?" asked Bedivere. "I

would think you'd want to keep it for yourself since it looks to be very expensive."

"I will admit only to the people in this room that it is crucial I give the gemstone to the king."

"What do you mean?" asked Willow.

"He probably means he has a purpose that is honorable and doesn't include doing or saying things only to manipulate people and situations," said Conrad, glaring at her.

Willow quickly turned away. She couldn't look into Conrad's eyes because if she did, she would want to kiss him again. What was the matter with her? She didn't even like him. Did she? "Earl Alnwick, I am sure you will be getting something of value in return," said Willow, ignoring Conrad's comment altogether.

"Well, that is yet to be seen," said the earl. "However, I hope to use it to save my castle. Ever since I found out King Richard has had his eye on this ruby for some time now, I thought it might keep him from giving my castle to John of Gaunt."

"You've got a border castle, don't you?" asked Conrad.

"I do. I had hoped to keep patrolling the borders and eventually make some alliances with the Scots. If John gets it, he plans on using it to start more battles. He holds no love of the Scots and would like nothing more than to kill them all."

"Then it's important that the king receives this ruby," said Willow. "It is worth much more than a castle, don't you think?"

"What price do you put on alliances that keep people from both sides from being killed?" asked the earl.

Willow decided the man was doing a very selfless thing. If it were her ruby, she would have a hard time handing it over for trade.

"May I?" Sir Bedivere reached out for the ruby, but the earl stopped her from giving it to him.

"I will take that back now," said Earl Alnwick, collecting the ruby from Willow. "I only wanted the young lady to know what it feels like to hold an expensive jewel in her hand. After all, she is the cousin of the king."

"Bastard cousin," Conrad pointed out, getting a glare from Willow.

The earl put the gemstone back into the chest and closed the lid. Then he took a key from his waist belt and locked the box, handing the chest to his guard.

"Thank you, Earl Alnwick, but I already know how it feels to hold an expensive jewel." Willow reached up and touched the jeweled crown that the queen had willed to her.

"That's some crown," said Sir George with a whistle.

"It was the late Queen Philippa's crown," she proudly told them.

"How did you get it?" asked Sir Chester.

"It was given to me –" She didn't finish because she couldn't tell them the real reason.

"What is that heart brooch you're wearing?" Sir Bedivere's finger reached out to trace it. It was an intimate act since she wore the brooch on her chest. His action took her by surprise, and she breathed deeply.

"Be careful, Bedivere, you might get slapped." Conrad stepped in between them, breaking the connection. "And I'm not talking about me."

"Gentlemen, will you join me in the great hall for some whisky?" asked Lord Beaufort. "I thought we could talk about the festivities for the morrow. After all, I'm sure you'll all be joining in the competitions."

"Not me. Now, if you'll excuse me, I'll escort the ladies back to their chamber," said Conrad. His words brought to mind the fact that his sister was standing at the back of the room. She'd been so silent, that Willow had nearly forgotten she was there.

"That's all right, I don't need an escort, Lord Conrad," Willow told him. "I am going down to the great hall, hoping for a dance or two before I retire for the evening."

"I'd like the first dance, my lady." Sir Bedivere gallantly held out his arm. Willow smiled. The man was handsome, and she wouldn't mind dancing with him. She reached out to take his arm but Conrad stepped in, and her hand came down upon his arm instead.

"I'm her guardian until her father returns to Rothbury," said Conrad. "She will not be attending the dance tonight I'm afraid, Sir Bedivere. Come, Hazel," he called out, holding out his other arm.

"Lord Beaufort," said Willow, looking to the man for help.

"He did make a deal with your father, Lady Willow."

Lord Beaufort shook his head. "Until Lord Rook returns, I'm afraid you will have to listen to Sir Conrad."

She had to change the earl's mind. There was no way she was going to bed so early when all the noblemen were below stairs. Well, she would just convince the earl to let her go. She had a way with him. "But Earl Rothbury, I'm sure you –"

"Good night," said Conrad, shuffling her out of the room.

"But Lord Beaufort." She looked over her shoulder, but Conrad dragged her to her own chamber. Once inside, he shut the door.

"How dare you!" shouted Willow, crossing her arms over her chest.

"You will stay here tonight and get to know my sister instead of getting to know all the men."

"What fun is that?" asked Willow with a pout.

"If I see you leave this room before morning, I swear I will drag you to Whitby Abbey by your hair and leave you there."

"You can't do that."

"I can. Your father gave me permission. As a matter of fact, it was his idea. So don't think I won't do it."

A knock was heard on the door. "My lord," came a voice from out in the corridor.

Conrad hurried over and opened the door to find his squire standing there.

"What is it, Toby?"

"Earl Rothbury, as well as Earl Alnwick, have sent me to fetch you."

"Fetch me?" asked Conrad.

Willow laughed. "I suppose they know you are dogging me. Perhaps, you should find yourself a nice bone in the kitchen and go chew on that for a while."

"They request your presence in the great hall to join them for some whisky. They are also making a list of which knights will compete in which events during the festival."

"I'm not going to be in any of them, didn't you tell them that? I have to watch over Willow."

"I'll let them know," said his squire.

"Nay," said Conrad. "I'll tell them myself. Willow, come here."

Willow smiled. "Oh, so you've changed your mind just like I knew you would. After all, the knights will want to dance with me." She picked up her skirts and hurried to the door, happy to be going to the great hall instead of to bed.

"Nay," said Conrad, stepping in front of her to stop her. He spoke in a low voice so only she could hear. "Please stop ignoring my sister. Would it kill you to talk to her and show a little kindness? She's just lost her mother and is feeling sad and very insecure."

Willow turned to look back at the girl who was standing next to the bed with her head down. She was the most pathetic young woman Willow had ever seen in her life. Her mousy brown hair was braided and coiled around the top of her head. She wore a short wimple that left her face in shadow. And her gown was the most unattractive, ugliest piece of clothing Willow had ever seen in her life. "Aye, I think it might kill me," she mumbled.

"If I see you down in the great hall, there will be hell to pay. Do you understand?"

"You know, I had hoped to have a dance with you, too, Sir Conrad. Perhaps I will let you have the first dance of the evening." She once again tried her tactics on him.

"Nay, you don't," he said, shaking his head. "Your little game may have worked on me once, but I swear your charming powers of persuasion will not work on me a second time. So save your breath."

She let out a sigh and looked back at his sister. "I don't want to stay here all night with her. She probably won't speak the entire time."

"You're so skilled with words that I'd think you'd be a good teacher. She needs you to guide her."

"Do you think so?" She looked up to see him smirking at her. "You didn't mean that, did you? You only said it because you were trying to manipulate me."

"You aren't the only one who can play that game." He smiled once more and turned and left the room.

Willow looked back at the quiet girl still standing there as if she were afraid to move. What could she possibly say to Hazel? And what could she teach the girl? It wasn't as if they had a thing in common. This was going to be the worst night of her life.

* * *

"My lord, you seem upset," said Toby as they made their way to the great hall. "Is something troubling you?"

"Aye, it's the girl," grumbled Conrad.

"Has Lady Hazel done something you don't like?"

Conrad stopped in his tracks and turned to talk to Toby. "Nay, it's not Lady Hazel I am talking about. She is too quiet for her own good, and that worries me. And leaving her with someone like Lady Willow does naught to ease my mind either."

"Ah, so it is Lady Willow who has you bothered."

"Aye, Toby, it is. I promised her father I'd watch over her and keep her away from the men, but that is already proving to be a full-time job."

"I can help you, my lord. Would you like me to keep an eye on Lady Willow?"

Conrad thought about it for a minute and shook his head. Lady Willow would have no trouble getting someone like Toby to do what she wanted. She'd barely even have to try. "Nay, it's my responsibility but thank you, Squire."

"There you are, Lochwood," said Earl Alnwick, sticking his head out of the great hall. "I didn't think you were going to make it down here in time, so I signed you up for the joust."

"You did?" Conrad wasn't excited about this. He already had his hands full with Willow and didn't have time to compete. "What made you think I'd be any good at it?"

"Come now, don't be so modest," said Alnwick, putting his arm around Conrad's shoulders as he headed into the hall. "Your squire told Earl Rothbury and me how no one can beat you at the joust. Plus, you are a knight, and he also mentioned you were mentored by one of the Legendary Bastards of the Crown. That's all we needed to hear."

"My squire told you that, did he?" Conrad tossed a frustrated glance behind him. Toby shrugged his shoulders and smiled. Conrad scoured the hall. "Where is Earl Rothbury?"

"He had to return to his solar, but he should be back any minute."

Conrad had some whisky with the earl, and then a tankard of ale as he waited for the lord of the castle to return. Finally, Lord Beaufort entered the great hall.

"Ah, Sir Conrad, I'm so glad you joined us. I wanted to talk with you," said Beaufort.

"What about?" Conrad had no idea what was going on.

"This year, the competitions are only for the single men, so I hope you will join us."

"Why only the single men?" he asked.

"Several lords are looking to marry off their daughters. And three winners will have the opportunity of choosing one of the eligible ladies of the castle to marry."

"Really?" His ears perked up. He wanted to marry and that had been part of the reason why he was here. Once he settled down with a wife, he'd bring Hazel to live with him. "I might be interested if the ladies are to my liking."

"Good, good," said the earl, ushering him to the front of the room. "I have the ladies of marrying age all lined up. There are three of them, and I think any of them would make you a suitable bride."

Conrad joined the other knights gathered around a table where the master of ceremonies had several lists with the competitors' names written down.

"Gentlemen," said the earl, holding his hand in the air. "I would like you to meet the ladies that will be married off to the winners of the competition. Their fathers have already spoken with me and agreed to the alliances of any of the knights, barons, and earls that I have invited here today. Actually, there will be three brides from which to choose."

"Three?" asked Sir Chester, walking up with a tankard of ale in his hand. "I only see two."

The earl looked up and shook his head. Then he summoned a page and sent him away. "The third lady will be here momentarily. In the meantime, I'd like everyone to meet Lady Anabel and Lady Grace."

Conrad joined the men to meet the ladies. Lady Anabel was a woman of only six and ten years, petite and blond. Lady Grace, on the other hand, was tall with red hair and seven and ten years of age. They were both very plain, but not ugly. He supposed they would make good wives.

"I'd like either one of them," said Sir Bedivere. "They both look like they'd be able to bear lots of sons for me."

"Nay, Sir Bedivere. Sir George and I want these two," Sir Chester told him. "You can have the last one."

"What last one?" asked Conrad. "I only see two."

"Oh, here she comes now," said the earl, flagging someone over.

Conrad turned around, and his jaw dropped open.

"Lady Willow!" he spat, not able to believe after he told her to stay in her chamber that she'd come down to the great hall after all. And to make matters worse, the earl was saying that she was one of the ladies up for marrying a winner of the games.

"Good evening, gentlemen." Willow curtseyed and held out her gown. Her presence in the hall took everyone's attention. She wore a gold taffeta gown with beading on the bodice. The skirt was lined with fancy lace. The back of her gown, instead of having buttons, was dropped low and he could see a flash of bare skin. And if that didn't get the attention of everyone there, then the crown on her head certainly did.

Conrad walked up and grabbed her by the arm. Leaning over, he whispered into her ear, "What do you think you are doing here? And dressed like that?"

"The earl summoned me," she said with a stiff upper lip. "I'm sorry, Sir Conrad, but his rank of nobility is higher than yours so there is naught you can do about it."

"Aye, I summoned her," said the earl.

"What's this all about?" asked Conrad.

"If you must know, I'm looking for a man to marry," said Willow. "I saw the earl headed to his solar and asked him to include me as one of the brides for the competitions."

"You did what? Nay." Conrad shook his head and held up his hands. "Earl, she can't be one of the prizes of your silly competition."

"Why not?" asked the earl. "She's old enough to marry. Past age, actually, so it is time she goes."

"I was asked by her father to be her guardian until his return," he explained. "Lord Rook will not like this."

Lord Beaufort nodded. "I thought so at first as well, but Lady Willow pointed out that she has the final say in whom she marries and that her father can't go against the wishes of the late king."

"You said that?" Conrad didn't know what to do with Willow.

"Well, it's true," she told him. "I was granted the right by my grandfather, the late King Edward III, to be able to agree to whom I marry. My father has no say in the situation at all."

The earl nodded. "Lady Willow does have that right."

"And I have the right to stop her until her father returns. It is my duty." Conrad couldn't let this happen.

"I'm sorry, Sir Conrad, but I take my orders from the king," the earl told him.

"That was an order given by a king who is no longer alive," Conrad pointed out. "It doesn't hold true anymore."

"You dare to question the word of your past king?" asked Lord Beaufort. "Sir Conrad, if you are going to fight this, then I will have to ask you to leave Rothbury."

Conrad studied the man's face. He meant what he said. Then he looked over to Willow who gave him a smug nod and proceeded to flirt with the other men that were guests at the castle. Nay, Conrad couldn't leave. Not now. Especially since he gave his word to Lord Rook as part of a deal.

He needed Hazel to be mentored in a castle, just like he was at one time. He also needed to keep an eye on Willow and keep her from these wolves that all looked as if they wanted to devour her. She was, by far, the prettiest of the three women. She was also the oldest. But he'd heard what the men thought of her. They might want her, but it would only be for a night of passion and pleasure. He couldn't let that happen. Her reputation preceded her, and none of these men would marry her because of it. However, they wouldn't bat an eye at taking her virtue.

"I'm not going anywhere, Earl Rothbury," he told the man, knowing now that he had to stay to stop this and there was only one way to do it. "Sign me up for all the competitions, not just the one. I think I'll find me a bride as well."

He glanced over at Willow, but she was no longer smiling. It was the only way to stop her from marrying one of the other men before her father returned. Conrad would have to win a competition and choose her as his bride.

CHAPTER 6

Willow lay in bed, dreaming of the kiss she shared with Conrad. But in her dream, he wasn't just kissing her. Nay. She was naked beneath him, and they were getting ready to make love! He fondled her breast and then reached down to kiss her there as well. She moaned aloud and turned over, liking the way her body vibrated. But then she suddenly had the feeling she was being watched. Her eyes popped open to find Hazel sharing her bed, looking at her with wide eyes.

"Oh!" she cried out, sitting up. "Why are you watching me like that?"

"You were making an odd noise," said Hazel. "Why?" she asked curiously, staring intently.

"Never mind." Willow yawned and stretched her arms above her head. She noticed Hazel staring at her chest. When her eyes roamed downward, she realized her nipples were hard. The dream had affected her in ways that were real. "Time to get up," she said, turning around and reaching for her clothes.

"What were you dreaming about?" Hazel asked in a soft voice.

If she were one of Willow's cousins, she'd tell her the truth. But how could she tell this young girl she'd dreamed of making love with Conrad? After all, the man was her brother. Oh, how she wished Maira or Fia were here right now.

"It doesn't matter," she said, pulling her gown over her head. "Dreams are silly and don't mean a thing."

"I often have dreams," said Hazel, pushing up and clutching the pillow to her chest. "So, are you telling me that they don't mean anything and that they will never come true?"

"Exactly," she said, putting on her hose and shoes. It worried Willow that she'd had an intimate dream about Conrad when she despised the man. There were so many nobles at the festival, but it was just her luck to be dreaming of Conrad the Cur. "Dreams are stupid and will never come true so don't even give them another thought."

"Oh." The girl's lips turned downward. She looked as if she were about to cry. Willow didn't know what to do.

"Why do you ask?" She stood up and reached for her boar's bristle brush, running it through her tangled hair. "What did you dream?"

"You said it doesn't matter." Hazel scooted to the edge of the bed and stood.

Willow felt awkward since she didn't know what to say

to the girl. Conrad's sister was young, and they had nothing in common. At least with Morag around, she never had to worry about conversation. Morag constantly did all the talking. But this girl was nothing more than a mouse. Since Willow didn't want to die of boredom, she decided to initiate the conversation. "Go on, Hazel. Tell me your dream." She continued to brush her hair.

"Do you really want to know?"

Nay, she didn't, but neither did she want silence between them. "I wouldn't have asked if I didn't care, would I?"

"I suppose not." That seemed to make the girl happy. She pulled her plain gown over her head and rushed over, climbing atop a chair. "I know it's silly but I sometimes dream I am a queen. Everyone bows down to me when I walk into the room."

"Hah!" Willow ran the brush through her hair, having had that dream once or twice herself. Unfortunately, she had to settle for noblemen bowing to her and just wearing the crown of a queen instead. "As I said, that is only a silly dream."

"I also dream that people notice me when I walk into a room and that they don't ignore me. People talk to me in my dreams and care about what I have to say. That's never going to happen, is it?"

"Huh?" Willow stopped brushing her hair, looking over to the girl, not really paying attention. There were tears in Hazel's eyes again. "Hazel, I don't really know a lot about dreams."

"Never mind. It's silly. And like you said, it'll never come true. People will never notice me the way they notice you, Willow." She got up and ran over to the bed, throwing herself atop it, crying.

Willow felt terrible having said those things to Hazel, making the girl cry. But that was before she realized that all the girl had was dreams. Willow wasn't good with situations like this. How she longed for Fia or even Morag to talk to. They would know what to say to Hazel to make her feel better. She let out a sigh and headed for the bed. She would have to make the best of this since it was partially her fault.

"Hazel," she said, sitting on the bed next to her. Hazel cried and hid her face in the pillow. "Hazel, look at me."

Slowly, the girl did so.

"If you want to be noticed, then you have to take control of the situation. It isn't going to happen on its own."

"What do you mean?"

"You poor dear. You really have no idea, do you?"

"Can you teach me to be like you, Willow?" The girl's eyes lit up in hope. Willow had no idea how to help her. "Mayhap a man will kiss me someday the way my brother kissed you."

"Oh." Willow's hand went to her chest, not expecting Hazel to say that. "That was a mistake. That's why I slapped him."

This conversation made Willow feel as if she were somehow being dishonorable by kissing the girl's brother.

She didn't do anything wrong. Did she? Willow's heart went out to her, remembering Conrad say that they had recently lost their mother. She was sure it couldn't be easy. Perhaps, she needed to show Hazel a little compassion.

"I want to be like you, Willow."

"Nay, you don't." Willow put her hand atop the girl's hand.

"Yes, I do. I want to be able to talk to the men easily, the way you do."

"It comes naturally for me, but I assure you it won't come to you as easily. You see, it's a talent that cannot be learned." Willow wasn't sure that was true, but she didn't want to teach this girl things that would only make Conrad angry with her. Nay, she would have to teach Hazel things like sewing and needlework or helping prepare herbs in the kitchen instead. The domestic skills that ladies were supposed to know. The only problem was, Willow was not good at any of those things. She had spent years avoiding the proper things expected of her that didn't make her happy. But Hazel was different. She was gentle, frail and weak. What was she going to do with her? And why did she have to be put in this position?

"Surely, there is some way you can help me."

"Well, mayhap there is," said Willow, deciding to do what she did best. "The first thing you need to do is let down your hair. Men don't like hair that is wound so tight that it makes your eyes look like slits. They also don't like when it's hidden beneath a wimple. That is for widows and old women."

"Show me," said Hazel, wiping away a tear from her cheek.

"All right." Willow reached out and unpinned Hazel's braid. "Let's brush out your hair and see how you look. I'm sure someone will notice the difference."

"Do you really think so?"

"Sure, why not? I wear my hair loose and long most of the time." She ran the brush through Hazel's hair.

"My brother says loose hair means the woman is loose as well."

She stopped brushing. "He does, does he? Well, he doesn't know what he's talking about."

"He also says that girls shouldn't approach a man and start talking to them, but rather wait to be approached by them first. It's not ladylike."

"Your brother has been teaching you falsities. None of that is true."

"He also says –"

"How about we go for a ride?" Willow didn't want to hear another word about whatever Conrad the Cur thought. She got up and took Hazel's hand, dragging the young innocent along with her.

"Where are we going?" asked Hazel as they headed for the door.

"We are going for a ride with the wind blowing through our hair and no one is going to stop us."

* * *

"BID THE DEVIL, Squire, why did you let me sleep so late?" Conrad hurried down the corridor, fastening his weapon belt around his waist as he walked.

"My lord, I tried to wake you, but you know as well as I that you sleep so soundly that the castle walls could come crumbling down around you and you wouldn't even know it."

"Stop exaggerating." Conrad headed toward Lady Willow's chamber.

"Your father used to say all the time that you'd probably sleep through your own wedding . . . as well as the consummation." Toby chuckled.

"That's not funny, Squire. Now, I'll hear no more. I might have times when I'm in a deep sleep, but I assure you I am still aware of everything that goes on around me."

"Of course, my lord."

"Now, there will be no word of this in front of Ladies Willow and Hazel."

"I understand."

"Willow. Hazel." Conrad rapped his knuckles against the door. "Open up. We're going to be late for the meal to break the fast."

"My lord, you've already missed that," Toby informed him. "The earl had the best quail eggs cooked in a buttery sauce and spicy herbs that were served over a thick slice of soft white bread." Toby smacked his lips. "I had two servings as well as some of the cook's special bilberry tarts."

"Bilberry tarts?" Conrad's head snapped up. He loved bilberry tarts. He used to take his mother berry picking.

They'd eat half the berries before they returned to the castle. This made him miss his mother dearly.

"And after that, there were two courses of –"

"That's enough," snapped Conrad. "If I want a report on every morsel of food served, I'll go down to the kitchen and ask the cook myself. Willow, open the door," Conrad called out, knocking again. When no one answered, he entered the room to find it empty. "Damn," he spat. "I've missed them. Were they in the great hall for the meal?"

"I'm not sure, but I don't think so," answered Toby. "Of course, when the servers came out with tray after tray of sweetmeats, cakes, fruit, cheese and even frumenty pudding, I have to admit I could focus on naught else."

Conrad salivated at the mention of all the food he'd missed while he slept. His stomach growled. He was so hungry he felt as if he could eat a horse. It angered him almost as much as the fact that Willow had snuck out without him.

"Come on, we've got to get down to the courtyard and try to find them."

After an hour of searching for the girls and not finding them anywhere, Conrad finally got his answer from a young man named Branton that happened to be Lord Beaufort's page.

"I saddled horses for Lady Willow and Lady Hazel early this morning," said the boy with a nod of his head. "They left well over an hour ago but have yet to return."

"Left?" asked Conrad. "What do you mean, left? They

can't have left the castle walls. I informed every guard on duty not to let Lady Willow leave here."

Branton smirked at hearing this.

"Why do you laugh?" asked Conrad, sternly.

"Because Lady Willow always leaves the castle unescorted."

"Unescorted? The women were by themselves?" The thought was unsettling. It was so dangerous for women to be outside the castle walls without a man to protect them.

"Aye, said Branton. "I offered to go with them, but Lady Willow said they wanted to go for a ride with the wind blowing through their hair. She said I would only slow them down."

"Wind through their hair? Willow is exposing my innocent sister to the ways of a harlot, I swear. How could this have happened?" Conrad paced back and forth in the courtyard. "They can't have gotten past the guards."

"They took the horses out the old postern gate. That's what Lady Willow and her cousins always do to avoid being seen exiting the castle."

"Egads, this is awful. Toby, saddle our horses, we've got to go look for them, anon."

"I wouldn't worry. They'll be back shortly," said Branton.

"How do you know that? Did they tell you where they were going?" Conrad drilled the boy with questions.

"Well, nay, but I can guess. I'm sure they went to the secret garden. That's always where they end up."

"Secret garden? What secret garden and where is it?"

"It was the garden of an old woman named Imanie who died last year."

"Why in heaven's name would she go there? Especially since the old hag is dead."

"I'm not supposed to say anything, but . . ." Branton looked around and then leaned forward and continued to speak in a whisper. "You know, Willow is one of the chosen ones by the late Queen Philippa."

"Chosen? Chosen for what? What in God's name are you talking about?" asked Conrad.

"She was their grandmother. The queen that is."

"I know that. Tell me something I don't know because you are trying my patience."

"The queen started a secret society of women called the Followers of the Secret Heart."

"Now I know you are making this up because it is the most outrageous story I've ever heard in my life. There is no such group and certainly not with women." He reached out and gripped the boy by the front of his tunic. "I'll teach you not to lie to me again."

"Sir Conrad, do not hurt my page because he tells the truth." The Earl of Rothbury walked across the courtyard to join them.

"I'm sorry, Lord Beaufort, but I find this whole idea of a secret group of women preposterous."

"Shhh." The earl leaned forward as well. "Not many of my men know about the garden and the secret organization. I'd like to keep it that way. After all, no man wants to hear how women are joining together to deceive us."

"Oh, I don't think they do it to deceive anyone, my lord," said Branton.

"Then what would they be joining together for?" Conrad's question was low and direct.

"We don't really know the answer to that," said the earl. "I don't believe even King Edward knew what the group was all about."

"If it is a true story then someone has to know about it," Conrad told him.

"Sir Conrad. I would rather turn a blind eye than to tell the girls' fathers that they are involved in such a group."

"Lord Rook doesn't know about this?" Conrad was surprised to hear that the earl kept it from Willow's own father.

"Nay, and you won't tell him," said Lord Beaufort. "After all, he and his brothers are the Legendary Bastards of the Crown. No one wants to get on their bad sides. Once the triplets' daughters are married and well cared for by noblemen, the happier they will be. That is one of the reasons I allowed Willow to put herself up as one of the brides for the competition. As she said, her father would feel confident if he knew she was married and had someone to look after her all the time."

"This is just too hard to believe." Conrad sheathed his blade.

"They have the queen's crowns as well as the heart brooches to prove it," said Branton excitedly.

Conrad shook his head in disgust. "Crowns and brooches or not, I promised Willow's father I'd look after her and I'll drag her back here by her hair if I have to. Where is this secret garden?"

"It's at the edge of the earl's lands," Branton relayed the information. "It's where the royal forest begins."

"Let's go," said Conrad, turning on his heel. His squire was right behind him.

"Wait, I'll come with you and show you how to get there." Branton raced to get his horse and returned immediately. "It's hidden in a cove and very hard to see. You'll never find it on your own."

"Believe me, I'd just have to follow the shine of Willow's crown and other jewelry to find her," grumbled Conrad. "I swear I'll tie her to the bedpost if I have to, but she'll not be taking my sister for unescorted rides in the woods ever again."

CHAPTER 7

"This garden is beautiful," exclaimed Hazel, slipping off her horse and heading toward the beds of overgrown flowers and weeds.

Willow wanted to share her secret place with Hazel so the girl would feel special. It was evident that she had a low self-image since she usually remained as quiet as a mouse and blended in with the wall. Even when she did talk, she kept her eyes focused on the ground.

At first, Willow wanted nothing to do with Hazel, but now she changed her mind. Undoubtedly, Hazel was pathetic, and that made her a challenge to work with. However, Willow liked challenges. She also secretly always wanted a sister. Being the only girl in the family made her feel lonely. She had her cousins, and they were close to her like sisters would be, but they weren't here now. She fancied the idea of having another girl to talk with.

Being taken away from Naward Castle and her family

at only the age of eight made her feel unwanted and invisible, just like Hazel. She knew what the girl was going through, and wanted to help her. Perhaps Willow's skills with people as well as with words could be beneficial in this situation.

"This is the secret garden of Imanie," Willow told her, tethering their horses and walking through the tall grass to join her.

"Imanie?" Hazel scanned the garden. "Is that her house?"

"Was," Willow corrected her. "Imanie was a mentor to me as well as my cousins, Maira and Fia."

"Where is Imanie now?"

"Right there." Willow pointed to the grave.

"Oh, no." Hazel held her hand over her mouth and made her way to the gravesite, falling to her knees. "It's so overgrown, I can barely see her grave marker." Hazel started pulling up weed after weed.

"Nay. What are you doing?" asked Willow, taking Hazel's hand and dragging her to her feet.

"Doesn't anyone care for the grounds now that's she's dead?" asked Hazel.

Willow surveyed the unkempt garden and shrugged. "Nay, I suppose not."

"Why don't you do it?"

"Me?" Willow laughed and brushed back a stray lock of hair. "Don't be silly. Gardening is a chore for servants, not noblewomen."

"I thought Imanie meant something to you."

"She did." Willow fingered Imanie's bracelet around her wrist.

"Then why don't you show her some respect by keeping up her garden now that she's gone?" Once again, Hazel dropped to her knees and started pulling weeds.

"Hazel, you are a noblewoman and shouldn't be doing this. Now get up."

"I will not." More tears flowed from her eyes as she pulled weeds faster and faster. "I lost my mother recently and wasn't even allowed to mourn her death before my brother dragged me away."

"I'm sure he did it for your own good."

"Did he?" She stopped pulling weeds and looked up. Anger showed in her eyes. "He came to Rothbury to leave me with Lord Beaufort, but even the earl doesn't want me. I'll end up in a nunnery someday because no one wants me near them."

"That's not true, now stop talking that way."

"Do you want me here?" asked Hazel, putting Willow on the spot. Willow hesitated, not sure how to answer.

"Mayhap I didn't at first, but now I don't mind the idea as much," she admitted.

"You don't want me, just say it." The girl put her face in her hands, trying to hide away from the world.

"Willow? Hazel? Are you here?"

Willow turned to see Branton entering the garden on horseback with Conrad and Toby right behind him.

"Branton, why did you bring them here?" she spat. "You know this is a secret place."

"Secret?" asked Conrad, dismounting. "Then why does half of Castle Rothbury know about it? Willow, why did you bring my sister here?"

"We wanted to go for a ride, that's all."

Conrad looked down at Willow, about to shake her for being so thoughtless. "You dare to take my sister outside the castle walls without an escort? Do you know how dangerous that is? What were you thinking?"

"Sir Conrad, I at least paid a little attention to your sister, when all you want to do is pawn her off on anyone who will take her," retorted Willow.

"That's not true."

"That's what Hazel said. Ask her yourself if you don't believe me. She feels unwanted."

"Hazel?" Conrad stepped around Willow and helped his sister to her feet. "You're crying. What did Willow do to you? And where is your wimple? Your hair isn't even in a braid." Conrad's blood boiled. What kind of a bad influence had Willow been on his dear, sweet, innocent sister?

"Willow said to do it, but I didn't want to." The girl sniffed and wiped away a tear.

"Now wait a minute, Hazel. That's not exactly the truth," said Willow.

"Why did you bring her here?" Conrad snapped at Willow. "This place is a tangled, twisted mass of weeds and overgrown plants. It is no place for a lady."

"I agree." Willow raised her chin and met him in challenge. "However, I wanted to show her a place that was at one time very special to me."

"This?" Conrad raised a brow, pulling his sister closer. "I'd be surprised if a wild boar didn't jump out trying to maul us."

"Conrad, I want to go back to the castle," said Hazel, sounding very upset. He put his arm around her and walked her to her horse.

"Let's go," he said, helping his sister mount. He looked up to see Willow settling herself on a wooden swing that was large enough for two. It hung from ropes between two shady trees. "I said, let's go, Willow."

"I will return later, so go ahead without me. I'm going to stay here for a while and pay my respects to Imanie." She fussed with her hair.

Conrad didn't want to argue with Willow since his sister was there. She was already so upset she was crying. It was surely from the fact that Willow forced her to ride unescorted and without a wimple. The poor girl was probably also frightened by the threatening look of these overgrown brambles.

"Toby, you and Branton escort Lady Hazel back to the castle. I will return with Lady Willow momentarily."

"Aye, my lord," answered Toby with a slight bow.

"Be sure to find a handmaid to tend to my sister's needs. And get her some wine to calm her nerves. She is very upset by this outing."

"We'll see to your sister," Branton assured him.

The three of them exited the garden, leaving Willow and Conrad alone.

"Why don't you go with them?" asked Willow in a calm manner. "I told you before, I don't need an escort or a guardian. There is no need for you to stay here with me."

"The way I see it, you need more than just an escort. What you need, Lady Willow, is a good turn over my knee and a swift slap of my hand against your bottom," growled Conrad. "What were you thinking to bring my sister here? You are very disrespectful."

"On the contrary, Sir Conrad, I'm being very respectful, but you can't see it. I came here not only to pay my respects to a dead woman, but I've also decided to help your sister. Now, why don't you sit down and stop lurking over my shoulder and brooding like a bear?"

"Lurking? Brooding?" He shook his head. He didn't lurk. Did he? And as far as he knew bears didn't brood. Was she saying she thought he was big and gruff like a bear? It made him wonder. She had him so shaken by her choice of words that he almost forgot he was in the midst of scolding her. "My sister doesn't need your kind of help."

One dark, thin brow raised in surprise. "Really? And what kind of help might you be referring to?"

Conrad sat down next to her on the swing. The ropes creaked under his weight, making him feel heavy. Like a bear. He tested a rope with his hand and then used his feet to give the swing a slight push.

"Oh," exclaimed Willow, falling back and into his arms. It wasn't a planned action, but he didn't mind the outcome.

She looked up at him, and all angry thoughts left his head. He found himself lost in her big, brown eyes. Willow Douglas had been a cute girl in her childhood, but now she was a raving beauty. Why did she have to be so pretty? It made it hard to discipline her the way her father wanted. When Conrad was near her, nothing else seemed to matter.

"Would you slap me if I kissed you again?" he asked, taking a chance but being cautious at the same time. Mayhap, if he asked her permission, she wouldn't be as eager to hit him like before.

"I might," she said, looking at his mouth. She wasn't pulling away, so he took that as a sign to continue.

"I'm willing to risk it," he mumbled, closing his eyes partially and lowering his mouth to hers. She seemed to welcome the kiss they shared. He welcomed it and craved more. The warmth from her body so close to his felt alluring. He lifted his hand and gently reached out to caress her shoulder. The contact between them had his senses reeling. Was this the same little girl he once taunted by pulling her braid and hiding frogs in her bed just to make her scream? Now the only screaming he wanted from her was to hear her crying out in ecstasy as he made sweet love to her and brought her to completion.

His head filled with fantasies and all of them involved the two of them in intimate positions. He couldn't think straight when he was around her. The whole damned thing almost seemed magical sitting on a swing with her in a secret garden. It was almost as if they were having a tryst, and damn if that didn't excite him. When she didn't push him away, he swept in for another kiss, this time reaching up with both hands caressing her shoulders with more intent.

"Mmmm," she said when he pulled away slightly, breaking the connection of their lips. With her eyes closed and her head tilted backward, it exposed her long, smooth neck. She also had a smile on her face – something he didn't expect to see. God's eyes, she was alluring. It wasn't just her beauty that intrigued him. Her spunk and determination were unlike any noblewoman he'd ever met. He liked that.

"Little Willow is all grown up," he whispered, reaching up to run his fingers against her cheek. He dipped down and kissed her on the neck next, running his hand through her loose tresses. But when his leather wristband snagged in her hair, he tried to get it free, ending up tugging at it in the process.

"Ow!" she said, springing up and pulling away. A few strands of hair clung to his wristband as they snapped by her abrupt movement. She pushed up from the swing. The smile and serene look she'd had on her face moments ago was gone. In its place was a frown and eyes that bore fire. "Conrad the Cur, I can't believe you're back to pulling my hair again just like you did when I was eight!"

He should have anticipated the slap that followed.

"God's eyes, I didn't do it on purpose." He jumped up to face her, but she was already halfway to her horse. "Where are you going?" he called out to her back as she picked up her skirts and stormed across the garden. "I thought you wanted to stay here to pay your respects to Imanie." Conrad rushed after her.

"I'm not the one who needs to show respect, Sir Conrad." With little effort, she pulled herself up into the saddle. "You wouldn't know how to treat a lady if your life depended on it."

With a turn of her horse, she kicked her heels into the animal's side and left him standing alone in the garden.

"Bid the devil, will this ever get any easier?" he grumbled as he mounted his horse. When Conrad made the deal with Rook to watch over Willow, he had no idea he'd be wasting so much time chasing after her.

* * *

WILLOW SPENT most of the day in the lists watching the noblemen who had come for the festival as they practiced for the competitions that would start on the morrow. She had hoped to spend time with Hazel, but the girl seemed to be sick and wanted to stay in bed the entire day. Willow wasn't about to stay locked in her room behind closed doors. That was the last place she wanted to be with so many noblemen roaming the castle. But every time she stepped foot outside of her room, Conrad was following her around like her shadow.

Earlier, when she left to visit the garderobe and to warm up her hands by the fire in the great hall, Conrad was there at her side or lurking over her shoulder. Even when she thought she'd managed to lose him when she ducked behind the mews earlier, she looked up to see him watching her from across the courtyard. She felt like a mouse being chased by a cat. She couldn't make a move without him knowing about it.

She contemplated sneaking away, but to do that she would have to avoid all the activities and she didn't want to miss anything. Willow had been waiting for this festival since last year and was not going to let Conrad ruin it for her. In the end, she decided her only option was to go places where Conrad could see her. As much as she didn't like the thought, at least she would be able to mingle with the other nobles.

Conrad's turn to practice the swordfight came up, and she oddly found herself mesmerized watching him.

He was no longer the lanky, awkward boy she once knew. Back then, he could barely hold a sword let alone swing it without taking out his eye. But now he effortlessly spun the blade around in one hand and brought it back to point at his opponent with accurate precision. Being drawn in, she watched as he challenged Lord Beaufort who was an excellent swordsman. Excitement grew in her belly. Part of her wanted to see him drop his sword. But after kissing him again, part of her secretly hoped he would have the better hand against the earl. "Go," she said, urging Conrad forward when Beaufort almost managed to unarm him.

"Quite skilled with the sword, isn't he?"

Startled, Willow looked up, not even realizing Sir Bedivere leaned on the rail of the lists next to her.

"I've seen better," she said, looking down and fingering her bracelet, not wanting to seem smitten with Conrad.

"You have?" That seemed to amuse Bedivere for some reason. "Well then, I'd like to know who you think is a better swordsman than your guardian."

"My guardian?" She wasn't sure at first if he meant Conrad or Beaufort since they were both serving as her guardian at the moment.

"He's not bad for his age. Not bad at all."

She looked back at the dueling men, realizing Bedivere thought she was supporting the earl. "Oh, the earl. Of course, not. No one is better."

"If you think so, then you haven't seen me with my sword in my hand." He reached out and covered her hand with his in a light squeeze. "Perhaps we can meet somewhere in private a little later? Your chamber?"

Her eyes shot downward. She didn't like him touching her. It didn't feel the same as when Conrad did it. When Conrad touched her, she welcomed it because it made her feel all tingly inside. When Sir Bedivere did it, it felt . . . dirty. This man wanted only one thing from her, and it was something she wasn't willing to give.

"How dare you suggest such a thing," she spat, pulling her hand away from him.

"All right, my chamber then. Or perhaps a tryst behind the barn is more to your liking?"

"Sir Bedivere, I'm willing to bet you will be very skilled with your sword in your hand just like you said. Only you will be holding your own sword all alone tonight because I wouldn't go anywhere with you." She purposely stepped down hard on his foot causing him to flinch and pull his hand off the rail.

Willow picked up her skirts and made her way through the lists with Sir Bedivere following her like a dog in heat. Looking over her shoulder at him, she wasn't watching where she was going and ran right into someone.

"Going somewhere, Lady Willow?" It was Conrad. He must have seen her leaving the lists and bee-lined it over to her. He breathed heavily from his practice, or perhaps from running over to head her off before she went. His sword was still clutched in his hand. Perspiration beaded his brow. She looked over her shoulder, and Sir Bedivere was smiling at her.

"Lochwood, I was just going for a walk with Lady Willow if you'll excuse us," said Bedivere.

He reached for Willow, but she quickly clasped her fingers around Conrad's forearm. "I'd like you to take me back to my chamber now, Sir Conrad."

"You would?" Conrad sounded surprised.

"Lochwood, get back on the field or the match will go to me," shouted Lord Beaufort.

"You'd better go," said Bedivere. "I can escort Lady Willow back to her bedchamber. After all, you can't disappoint the earl."

"Nay, she's my responsibility. I'll take her." Conrad's words caused Willow to draw a breath of relief. "You take my place on the practice field, Bedivere."

"Aye," said Willow. "Perhaps, Sir Bedivere, you can get in some practice, holding your sword after all."

Bedivere gave her a disgruntled look and ducked under the lists, making his way to spar with the earl.

CONRAD ESCORTED Willow through the courtyard, and then up the stairs to her chamber.

"I'm surprised you wanted my protection from Bedivere when you so blatantly slapped me again earlier."

"Me? Oh, that," she said, sounding as if she'd almost forgotten all about it.

"What happened between you and Bedivere that had you so spooked?" He'd seen Willow in action. She wasn't one to shy away from any man. If she was running from Bedivere and straight into his arms, there was a reason.

"Nothing happened." She flashed a smile.

"You were playing with fire again, weren't you, Willow? If you keep that up, eventually you will get burned."

"For your information, I was doing nothing of the sort. I was merely watching you practice when Lord Bedivere put his hand over mine and made a crude suggestion."

"What?" He stopped in his tracks, a vein throbbing in his neck. "Tell me what he said and I'll have his head, I swear I will."

"Conrad, calm down. Nothing happened. That is all that matters."

"Nay! What matters is that men are lusting after you, and I don't like it."

"Lusting?" She blinked her eyes, her lashes like the wings of butterflies as they flitted up and down. Even that was graceful about her. "Is that what you think?"

"It's what I know. Every man here only wants one thing from you, Willow. And with the way you lead them on, you are going to get yourself into trouble."

Her hand slipped from his arm, and her face became stone-like. "Is that why you kissed me? Do you lust after me as well?"

"Nay, that's different," he tried to explain, although it wasn't looking good for him.

"How is it different? I don't see it as being anything other than lust just like you are accusing the other men of doing. You are no better than them."

She reached for the door, but Conrad stopped her with his hand on hers. "Willow, I might lust for you, I'm not going to lie. You are a beautiful woman, and no man in his right mind wouldn't want you. But I'm not like the others."

"Like the others?"

"They only want to take you to bed. They don't care about you the way I do."

"You only care about me because my father has made a deal with you."

"Nay that's not true. I've known you for a long time, and these men haven't. Yes, I've sworn to protect you, but the other men are different."

"I don't see it."

"Open your eyes, Willow. They want you for pleasure only, not to marry."

Her face turned upward, and her eyes became glassy. He could tell that his careless choice of words cut her deeply.

"What do you mean that no one would want to marry me? What are you saying? That I'm not good enough for any man to want as his wife?"

"Nay, I didn't mean it like that."

"That's what you said."

"I was only trying to stress the fact that . . . I mean that . . ."

"What? Spit it out, Sir Conrad, or have your lies and unkind words lodged in your throat and threatened to choke you like I want to do to you right now?" She turned and opened the door. He couldn't let her leave this way. Without thinking, he blurted out, "I want to marry you, Willow."

She stopped and turned around and cocked her head.

"What did you say?"

"I said – I'm competing in the tournament."

"Nay, that's not what you said." She shook her head and narrowed her eyes. "You said you want to marry me. Is that true?"

Conrad swallowed the lump in his throat. His mouth felt so dry he didn't think he could speak if he tried. He had joined the competition just to bide time until Lord Rook returned. He figured if he won and chose her for his wife, he could manage to keep her away from the other men and, at the same time, stall until her father's arrival. He hadn't really considered her the type of wife he had hoped to find. But after that last kiss, he couldn't see himself with anyone else but her.

"Willow, I . . ."

"Never mind," she spat. "I know you think of me as naught but a loose woman since I wear my hair unbraided."

He shook his head in surprise. "Why would you say that?"

"That's what Hazel told me. She also said you think women who talk to men before spoken to are not ladylike at all. Don't try to pretend you want to marry me because I know what you really think of me."

"But I do . . . want to marry you." There, he said it, and it felt right.

"Forget it," she said.

"What did you say?" He couldn't have heard her right. Shouldn't she be thrilled that someone wanted to marry her? After all, that is why she put herself up as a prize bride for the competition.

"I said, forget it. I have been granted permission by the late king to agree to whomever I am to marry. And I'll tell you right now, Conrad the Cur, I would not marry you if you were the last man on earth." She disappeared into the room and slammed the door in Conrad's face.

"My lord! There you are." Toby hurried down the corridor to join him. "I've been looking for you. The practice for the joust is about to begin. Why aren't you out on the field? I have your horse, as well as the lances prepared."

"I'm not going," he said, turning and heading down the

passageway in a huff. His encounter with Willow didn't go at all as planned.

"Not going?" Toby followed behind him. "Why not?"

"Because I've had enough jousting today and I'm finished."

"You have? When? I didn't see you on the tiltyard."

Conrad stopped so quickly that Toby knocked into him from behind. "I didn't joust on the tiltyard, Squire."

"Then where did you joust?"

"Put it this way. Never joust with a beautiful woman with a mind of her own who twists your words into something they're not because she will always be triumphant in the end."

CHAPTER 8

"*H*azel, you have barely stepped foot out of this chamber in the last two days," chided Willow. "You can't stay hidden away in here feeling sorry for yourself forever."

"I'm not feeling sorry for myself." Hazel clung to the bedpost like a lifeline and stared at the floor.

"Then what do you call it?" Willow dressed for supper, choosing a burgundy gown made of velvet. There were ruffles of lace on the bodice and at the bottom of the long tippets as well. Her handmaid, Clara, helped her. But most of the time, Willow dismissed the woman, not wanting a handmaid at all. The woman only seemed to get in her way. She and her cousins had always helped each other. None of them felt they needed a personal servant.

"I'm not feeling well, that's all." Hazel walked over to the window and peered out.

It about broke Willow's heart that the girl was so glum. Conrad didn't seem to notice. He kept busy practicing for the competitions that started on the morrow. Tonight was the festival of light. Lanterns and torches would be lit in the castle courtyard, outside the castle gate and even on the path leading through the woods. There would be a giant bonfire constructed just outside the castle for everyone to enjoy. Strolling musicians would play music, and the visitors would dance out in the elements as they drank wine, whisky, and ale.

Vendors from many towns would be here today as well as late into the evening. This was going to be a huge celebration and one she didn't want to miss.

"How about if you and I choose what we'll wear for the festival tonight?" Willow tried her best to cheer up Hazel. "Where are all your clothes?"

"I only brought with me what's in my trunk." Hazel pointed to a trunk in the corner that Willow forgot was even there.

"I'm sure we'll find something in here that will make you feel beautiful." She walked across the room and flipped open the lid.

"Nay, please don't look at my things."

The girl was even shyer than Willow had thought. Either that or she was embarrassed, and Willow could see why. As she dug through the gowns and shoes, everything was so ugly that Willow wouldn't be caught dead wearing any of it. It only took a quick perusal of her things to realize this wasn't going to work. "Where are all your good gowns? The ones you wear for dances and on special occasions? Did you leave them back at your castle?"

"You mean the manor house," she said. "And no, I don't go to dances or attend special occasions, so there is no need for me to have fine gowns like you have."

"Conrad doesn't have a castle?" This surprised her more than the fact that Conrad never bought his sister a beautiful gown. Willow had thought he'd have a castle and was disappointed to hear that he only had a small manor house after all.

"My family is not rich like you, Willow."

"Oh," she said, not knowing how it felt to be poor. She always had everything she needed living with the earl. Even when she was a child, her father made sure to spoil her.

"Those are all the gowns I have."

Willow pitied Hazel. After all, every woman needed to have nice things. She had the feeling that Hazel had never known that and nor would she know it in this lifetime. Living with the earl, and being the granddaughter of a king, Willow had always been taken care of, even though her father was naught but the king's bastard. Well, she decided, someone needed to take care of Hazel, too. She had no parents, and her only brother didn't seem to watch over her half as much as he did Willow. She slammed down the lid and stood up, brushing off her hands.

"If you don't have anything appropriate to wear to the

festival tonight, then we'll find you one of my gowns to wear instead. I think we probably wear the same size."

Willow grabbed Hazel's hand and pulled her to the adjoining wardrobe. It was a small room attached to her bedchamber where she kept her clothes and other personal items. After lighting a beeswax candle, she led Hazel inside.

"What's this?" asked Hazel, stopping in the doorway and taking in her surroundings. "There are so many gowns and shoes that this must be where all the ladies of the castle keep their clothes."

"Nay, these belong to just me." Willow walked over and pushed a few of her hanging gowns aside, choosing one that was pretty, but not too ornate for the girl to wear. After all, Willow wanted to look the best at the festival. She didn't want anyone to outshine her even though Hazel could never do that. "We'll try this one," she said, holding it up in the air to show the girl.

"That one?" Hazel reached out and touched it lightly. "It's such a bright color."

"It's dark green," Willow told her. "There's nothing bright about it. Besides, you want everyone to notice you so this will help you stand out."

"I'm not sure that my brother would approve of it. The bodice is so . . . low."

"Nonsense. It's not low at all." Willow held the gown up in front of her to show Hazel. The bodice did show some cleavage but wasn't nearly as low as many of her other gowns. "You're just used to having a gown that is up to your neck, that's all. I'm surprised you can breathe at all since your clothes look so restricting. Now believe me when I say it'll get you noticed and make you feel pretty as well. Try it on."

"I'm not sure," said Hazel, her eyes fastened to the gown. Willow could see the way her eyes lit up with excitement and awe when she looked at it. She could also see that Hazel was afraid of what Conrad would say.

"I'll make sure to talk to Conrad, so don't worry about him. He'll agree with it," she tried to reassure her.

"Do you really think so?"

"There isn't a man yet I haven't been able to convince of anything. Aye, I'm sure."

"All right then."

Willow took it as a challenge to make Hazel into the lady she was meant to be. When she got done with Conrad's sister, no man would ever ignore her again.

* * *

CONRAD PACED BACK and forth in the courtyard, waiting for Willow and Hazel to join him. Being the girl's guardian was proving to be much more of a chore than he thought it would be. Lord Beaufort kept him busy practicing, drinking, and talking with the men for much of his time. Conrad couldn't deny the earl his request since he was the host of the festival. But because of it, he wasn't watching Willow the way he should be. He also hadn't seen much of Hazel lately, and that bothered him. Hazel was so shy that she was spending most of her time in Willow's chamber hidden away. She wasn't a typical girl and had many problems. She often acted in ways that could prove to be troublesome. Conrad couldn't wait for Lord Rook to return, to serve as the girl's guardian and mentor. Perhaps the man's wife would be able to bring his sister out of her shell and get to the root of her problems.

"I cannot believe it is taking them this long to change their clothes," Conrad complained to his squire. "Mayhap, I should go up there and drag them down here myself. It's already nightfall. The festival of lights is starting."

The courtyard was filled with people from nobles to servants and even merchants and serfs. Tonight was the part of the festival where everyone stayed up till the wee hours of the morning, celebrating, dancing, eating, drinking, and making merry. It was also the time when the competitors could get to know the prize brides and decide which one they wanted to compete for to win her hand in marriage. The bonfire would take place outside the castle gates but far enough away from the travelers' tents that were pitched, lining the area just outside the castle.

"Lochwood, have an ale with us. You look uptight," said Lord Beaufort. He and Earl Alnwick approached with tankards of ale in their hands. Pie vendors, alewives, jugglers and merchants from town filled the area. Small children chased after a barking dog while nobles tossed coins to some of the children or beggars outside the gate.

"Two pies for a penny," said an old woman with a tray of small fruit pies that were only the size of one's hand. She picked up a bilberry pie and held it in front of Conrad's nose. The fruity aroma wafted up making him salivate.

It smelled delicious and was one of his favorite things to eat, but he needed to look for Willow and stay at her side. He needed to focus. "Nay," he said, dismissing her with a wave of his hand.

A group of men, mostly nobles and knights, caused a ruckus just outside the keep. Conrad couldn't see what was going on, but the men were all crowding around in a circle. They were becoming rowdy, and he wasn't sure a rumble wouldn't start soon.

"If you'll excuse me," he said to the earls. "I need to find Lady Willow."

"I don't think you'll have to look too far," Toby told him, stretching his neck to see over the crowd of people.

"What do you mean?" he asked.

"Look." Toby pointed to the group of discordant men. Conrad glanced over at the men. His mouth dropped open. As the group parted, Willow emerged from the center. She wore a burgundy gown that clung to the sensuous curves of her body, leaving little to the imagination. Her hair was loose and hung down around her shoulders, looking shiny in the firelight of the torches. Queen Philippa's crown was balanced precariously on her head, the jewels winking as she strolled across the courtyard laughing and talking in a singsong voice. The men followed her around like puppies.

"Willow," he said in a low voice, not liking what he saw. Her bodice showed cleavage that he could see all the way from across the courtyard in the dark. It was like a beacon signaling every man there as if she were advertising her wares. "Nay you don't," he growled, storming across the courtyard, ready to wring her neck. "Lady Willow, I'd have a word with you."

She looked up; her big, brown eyes drawing him in like a moth to a flame. The firelight of all the torches lining the area made her skin glow. She was the shining vision of loveliness, and he couldn't deny it.

"Why, there you are, Sir Conrad," she said in a sweet voice – too sweet of a voice that he was sure wasn't meant for him. "We were looking for you."

"We?" He didn't understand who she meant until Willow walked back into the crowd of men and pulled someone along with her. "Don't be shy, Hazel."

"Hazel?" If Conrad wasn't shocked by what he'd already seen, he most certainly was now.

His sister, Hazel, emerged from the crowd of men, holding Willow's hand. For a minute, he didn't think it was really his sister because he almost didn't recognize her.

"Hello, Conrad." Hazel's voice was soft. She looked up meekly but kept her face turned toward the ground. She wore a flowing green gown with her breasts trussed up like a Christmas goose. Her hair was loose like a strumpet's and blowing in the wind. No wimple covered her head, leaving her exposed to the elements and the eyes of every man there. And around her neck was a jeweled bauble that reminded him of a dog's collar. She lifted her hand in a small wave, the bracelets around her wrist jangling as she did so. She wore a ring on almost every finger, and her nails even seemed to shine.

"Hazel!" he spat, pushing through the crowd, grabbing his sister's arm and pulling her toward him. "Get away from them. And why are you dressed like a bloody gypsy?"

"What are you doing, Lochwood?" asked Sir George. "We were just getting to know Lady Hazel."

"When did she arrive?" asked Sir Bedivere, stretching his neck to see her, collecting two goblets of wine off a server's tray and handing one of them to Hazel. "Have some wine, Lady Hazel. I'd like to escort you to the festivities tonight."

"She'd like that," said Willow with a nod, speaking for the girl. "Wouldn't you, Lady Hazel?"

"Well I . . ."

"Nay, she wouldn't!" Conrad interrupted. "The only place you will be escorted, dear sister, is back to the bedchamber to change into more appropriate clothes."

"Conrad." Willow pulled him to the side. "Let her have some fun. She's being noticed for the first time in her life."

"Aye, but for all the wrong reasons. Let's go, Hazel." He held on to her arm, starting back to the keep. But Willow's voice from behind him made him stop in his tracks.

"I've had so many of you offer to escort me to the festivities tonight, that I might just have to close my eyes and point to one of you to make my choice."

"Here, use this as a blindfold," offered Sir Chester, pulling a cloth from his pocket. "Then you can choose fairly."

Conrad groaned. If he took Hazel back to the bedchamber now, Willow would have gotten into trouble before he returned. Nay, he had to stay at her side since it is what he promised her father. "Toby, take Lady Hazel back to the keep and then escort her to the festival after she's changed into proper attire."

"Aye, my lord," answered Toby.

"But I'm ready for the festival now," said Hazel.

"Not looking like that you're not!"

"Willow told me this would get me noticed."

"Aye, and that is the problem. You don't want to be noticed in that way."

"I don't understand." Hazel held out her gown and looked down. "Don't you like the gown? It's one of Willow's."

He did like the gown, but not on his sister. Willow was proving to be a bad influence on the girl. This had to stop immediately.

"Hazel, I won't tell you again. Go back to your chamber and change your clothes before you return to the festival."

"You don't care about me, Conrad. You don't want me to enjoy myself," wailed Hazel. "Well, don't worry because I'm not returning to the festival at all." She ran off before Conrad could reply. He took a step to go after her but stopped when he heard Willow giggle. Then half a dozen men laughed as well. This could only end up being trouble.

"See to my sister," Conrad told his squire. "I'm going to attend to Lady Willow before she ends up in a bad place."

"Aye, my lord." Toby took off at a run.

Conrad turned back, making his way through the crowd.

"I'm going to spin around with my eyes closed and whoever I point to is the lucky man who will be my escort for the night." With a blindfold over her eyes, Willow spun in a circle with her arm extended while all the men there cheered her on.

"Get out of my way," Conrad snarled, pushing a few men to the side, stopping right in front of her.

"I choose . . . you," said Willow, giggling as she made her decision. With her arm extended and finger pointed, she stopped and pulled off the blindfold.

"Congratulations, Lady Willow," he told her with a sarcastic grin. "It seems I am to be your escort for the evening after all."

Her smile turned to a frown very quickly when she realized she was pointing right at Conrad.

"Let me try again," she said, raising the blindfold to her eyes.

"There is no need because I will make sure I am standing in front of you every time. Now conduct yourself like a lady and join me at the festival of lights." He held out his arm and waited for her to take it. Willow dropped the blindfold to the ground and gripped her talons into his arm. She smiled at the rest of the men and nodded as they headed away.

As soon as they were out of earshot, she let him have it. "Do that again, and next time I'll poke out your eyes with my pointing finger." Her words held venom as the two of them made their way through the crowd, but the phony smile never left her face as she nodded at one nobleman after the next acknowledging all of them but him in a friendly manner. This was going to be one of the longest nights of his life.

CHAPTER 9

With Conrad's arm around her shoulders to keep her warm, Willow anticipated watching the dancing flames of the bonfire happening now outside the castle's gate. The nighttime festivities were starting, and Willow was anxious to be a part of it all. At first, she had hated the fact Conrad was her escort tonight. She didn't think she would have a chance to talk to any of the single noblemen, but that proved to be wrong.

"Sir George," said Conrad, holding a goblet of wine in one hand, and keeping his other arm around her shoulders as they strolled through the courtyard. A crowd of merchants had their tables set up along the wall of the keep. They had been selling their wares all day. As the sky grew dark, they lit torches and lanterns hoping to make more sales during the nighttime hours.

"Lochwood, I came over here to get acquainted with the

bride-to-be." Sir George bowed and reached out for Willow's hand.

"Sir George, that is so kind of you." Willow extended her arm, letting the man kiss the back of her hand. Conrad's hold on her shoulders tightened in what she knew was a silent warning of saying he didn't like the kiss and that it was lasting too long.

"That's enough, Canterbury," Conrad remarked, clearing his throat.

"What's the matter, Lochwood? Jealous that I'm kissing your girl's hand?" George chuckled.

"I'm not his girl," Willow stated, wanting all the men to know she was still available to marry.

"Nay, I'm not jealous." Conrad nodded to someone behind him. "It's just that Ashington and Gaunt want their turns as well."

Willow turned to see Sir Chester and Sir Bedivere approaching from the midst of the crowd.

"Ah, there you are, Sir Chester. I wondered where you'd disappeared to," said Sir George.

"I've been busy this morning." Sir Chester kissed Willow's hand next. "Sir Bedivere, I waited for over an hour for you in the great hall, but you never showed."

"Good evening, Lady Willow." Sir Bedivere kissed her hand next. When he touched her, Willow cringed but didn't pull away since it wouldn't be polite. "I don't know what you're talking about Sir Chester, I was waiting at the mews for you," Bedivere told him.

"We were supposed to meet in the great hall."

"My mistake. I suppose I was too engrossed in talking with the Ladies Anabel and Grace and must have forgotten. I do think any of the three ladies would make fine wives. Don't you think so, Lochwood?"

"Mmmph," Conrad grunted, taking Willow's arm and escorting her away toward the stable. "Excuse us, my lords, but Lady Willow and I are going for a ride."

"We are?" Willow looked back over her shoulder at the other men as Conrad guided her to the stable. "It's the middle of the festival and the dancing is about to start. Why on earth would we go for a ride now? After all, we won't see much in the dark."

"Come, Willow," was all he said, helping her to mount his steed that wasn't even saddled.

"Wait," she said, as his hands encompassed her waist and he lifted her atop the horse. "This horse isn't prepared for an outing."

"It'll be easier for the both of us to ride without the saddle." He climbed up behind her and reached around her for the reins.

"My lord, where are you going?" Toby bolted into the stable grabbing a saddle. "Let me saddle the horse for you and Lady Willow."

"Toby, there's no need. Now please keep an eye on my sister until our return."

"But my lord, I became tired of sitting outside her chamber door, with her never emerging," complained Toby. "I thought, perhaps, if Lady Hazel isn't going to get out of bed, I might be able to grab a bite at least to eat and enjoy some of the activities."

"Take an hour and no more. And then back to your post. I want someone here for her if she decides she's feeling better and wants to join the celebration."

"When will you return?" asked Toby, fidgeting with the saddle.

"I'll return when I'm good and ready, now stop asking so many questions."

"I'd like to know the answer to that, too," Willow broke in. "After all, tonight is the only time I might have to mingle with the eligible noblemen. If I can't talk to them and get to know them, how am I going to choose one to marry?"

"You're not choosing any of them," Conrad told her, directing the horse from the stable.

"I have the right to agree to whom I marry," Willow reminded him. "It was the late queen's wish and the command of King Edward on his deathbed as well."

"If I must remind you; the man who wins the competition will choose you, and you can either say aye or nay. That is the extent of it."

"But how am I going to know if I should agree to a marriage or not? I demand you turn this horse around and take me back to the bonfire. I want to talk to more of the noblemen who will be competing for my hand."

"There's no need for that," said Conrad, heading over the drawbridge. They rode past the noisy crowd that laughed and conversed while the musicians strolled through the area playing music and some of them singing to whoever would listen. The jester entertained a group of children by doing tricks with a deck of cards. There were pitched tents boasting the coat of arms of many knights filling the entire area. This was where the travelers stayed who weren't lucky enough to occupy a room in the castle. The bonfire glowed brightly from the center of the ring of tents. Willow wanted more than anything to stay and enjoy herself. However, Conrad took it upon himself to decide they should go for a ride instead. Of all times, why now?

"Sir Conrad, I don't want to go riding in the dark. I want to stay at the festival. Now, please turn around and take me back to the castle. I need to talk to the competitors to decide which one I will marry."

"I told you before, and I'll tell you again. There is no need to worry your pretty little head about that."

"Why not?" she asked, feeling as if she already knew the answer. "Is it because you believe I'm perceived as a strumpet and not one of the men will want me for his bride?"

"That's not true. I don't think you're a strumpet. And don't worry yourself with what the others will think of you since you won't be marrying any of them."

"You don't know what you're saying."

"On the contrary, it is you who doesn't understand."

"Then why don't you tell me what you mean?" Willow tired of this conversation.

"Let me remind you, I'm competing as well."

"I know that. But what does it have to do with any of this?"

"I am going to win at least one of the competitions. And you, Lady Willow, will be my wife."

"Your wife? Hah!" Willow spat out the words thinking the man had gone mad. "Why would you even think I'd consider marrying you, Conrad the Cur?"

"Don't call me that." His arm stiffened around her waist, and he rode faster, heading through the forest.

"Why are you doing this?" His actions, as well as his words, aggravated her more than she let on.

"It is a beautiful night, and I know how much you like sneaking out in the dark."

"Not that. I mean why are you competing for my hand in marriage?"

"I need a wife."

"There is always Lady Anabel or Lady Grace. Perhaps you can choose one of them instead." She tried to get him to change his mind.

"They are too young."

"They're basically the same age as me," she pointed out.

"You seem much older." He directed the horse toward the secret garden. Even in the dark, Willow knew this route since she'd taken it with her cousins to see Imanie many times in the past.

"So you're saying you think I'm too old for anyone to want to marry me?"

"Nay. I'm not saying that at all. I just meant . . . you are more mature."

"Mature in what way? You're not referring to me being a strumpet again are you?"

"Willow, what I mean is –"

"Because if you are, I'll –"

"I am starting to have strong feelings for you," he said, keeping her from finishing her sentence.

His words surprised her so much that she didn't know how to respond. First, he said he wanted to marry her, and now he was admitting to having feelings for her. What could this mean? And did she feel the same way? She didn't think so. But the more she thought about the kisses they'd shared, the more she wondered what it would be like to be his wife. Part of her wanted to get to know Conrad after all.

"You're taking me to Imanie's secret garden, aren't you?" she asked, rather than having to respond to what he'd just told her.

"Aye." Conrad gave a quick nod of his head. "You said you wanted to pay your respects to Imanie the other day. However, you left so fast that you didn't get the chance."

"I suppose so," she answered, almost wishing he had said he was coming here because he wanted to spend time with her alone. Then again, what did it matter? They weren't meant for each other, she reminded herself. To her, he'd always be the boy who pulled her braid and hid frogs in her bed. He would always be naught else but Conrad the Cur.

They entered the garden and stopped right inside the gate. The moon lit up the surroundings making everything seem so surreal. Imanie's house sat lonely and empty across the garden. The stall that once held her horse was empty, too. At her death, the girls brought the horse to the castle and Morag claimed it.

Weeds choked out the flowers that came back year after year on their own. Where once this was a place of solitude and safety, now Willow felt as if it were naught more than a place for evil to lurk in the shadows. With Imanie gone, it seemed as if her years of mentoring were naught but a dream. She found her thoughts drifting back to the time when Imanie taught her that she was more than just a pretty face. She had skills and talent as well.

"You are a bright girl, and prettier than most women," said Imanie.

"Do you really think so?" asked Willow.

"I'm sure you have made many noblemen feel good about themselves, just by being on their arm at a dance or festivity."

"I don't really care to dance, and don't talk to men much unless they talk to me first."

"Now, I know that is a lie. I've heard your cousins say how much you like the men. If you are going to try to trick me, you need to make it sound more convincing."

"I'm not trying to trick you, and neither do I want to deceive anyone."

"Of course not. But if you are going to be a member of the queen's Followers of the Secret Heart, you might be required to do things you've never done before."

"So, you're saying I will need to lie?"

"Nay, I'm not saying that at all. But when the time comes to help your country or your fellow man, you will need to make a decision and stick with it. No matter what it might be."

"Do you think I can really do that, Imanie?"

"I think you can accomplish whatever you set out to do. You have a way of saying things that make men – or anyone listen. I've heard you convince your cousins of doing many things in the past that they had no intention of doing. It was easy for you. Embrace who you are, Willow. Don't be afraid of it. Fear will only hurt you in the end."

"I wish I could be brave, but I'm not sure I can."

"Of course you can. But I must warn you. Always be sure to really want what you wish for because you might get it. And sometimes it isn't at all what we'd hoped it would be."

"I still don't know how to use my skills for anything helpful or for a good purpose."

"You'll know when the time comes."

"But what if I don't? What if there is something important I need to convince someone of and I can't do it?"

"If it isn't working, then use the element of surprise to catch them off guard. That always works."

"Element of surprise," she said, pondering the idea and wondering if it would really work.

"Lady Willow?"

Willow was dragged from her thoughts by Conrad's voice from the ground. She looked down from the horse to see him with outstretched arms, waiting to help her dismount. The moonbeams gave a bluish cast to his dark, oaken hair that was almost black. Brown eyes reflected in the midnight sun, making him look devilishly handsome as well as dangerous. Somehow, getting her braid pulled by him didn't seem so treacherous anymore. She was alone with a handsome man in a secluded garden at night. What if he tried to ravish her? Would she fight him? Or would she welcome his advances?

Holding out her arms, she felt his hands close around her waist as he helped her from the horse and slid her down his body to the ground. A delicious shiver of anticipation swept through her. When he looked down into her eyes, she found herself wanting to kiss him again. And when he reached out to touch her chin, she was sure he was going to press his lips against hers. Instead, he brushed his hand against her and dropped his hand to the side.

"You had a smudge on your face," he told her, turning away quickly to look at the garden. "Now, where was that grave?"

CONRAD KNEW PRECISELY where Imanie's grave was but needed an excuse to turn away from Willow before he did something he would regret. After touching her, he almost kissed her again. At the last minute, he pretended to be brushing away some dirt from her cheek instead. He needed to be careful when it came to Lady Willow. Lately, his feelings for her were getting stronger. He couldn't believe he'd admitted he felt anything for her at all. And to his disappointment, she didn't even seem to care. One kiss in a dark, secluded garden could tempt him to want to do so much more. He promised her father he'd keep her away from the men. He was sure that included him, too.

They made their way across the garden, his hand on the small of her back to guide her and keep her from tripping in the dark. The moonlight lit up their surroundings enough for them to see.

"It's over here," she told him, leading the way to Imanie's grave. The wind picked up, swaying the branches of the trees overhead. The scent of rain suddenly made the air heavy.

"I think there's a storm coming," he said, perusing the sky. "Perhaps you'd better pay your respects quickly. We'd better leave before we're caught in the rain."

"I'm sure we have plenty of time yet," she said in a care-free manner. "After we pay our respects, I'd like to show you something in the house."

He glanced up at the sky again. A flash of lightning lit up the horizon. Thunder rumbled lowly in the distance. They didn't have long before the storm approached.

They hadn't been at Imanie's grave for more than a minute when Willow's head snapped up, and she grabbed hold of his arm.

"That's good," she announced. "This way, please." She directed him to the cottage, holding tightly to his arm as they climbed the two small stairs leading up to the porch. "There is an oil lantern we can use, right inside the door."

He followed her into the house, waiting while she lit the lamp. The firelight cast a soft orange glow in the one-room structure. Conrad looked around to see dusty furniture atop an old water stained, wooden floor. Besides the dust and musty aroma, the place looked as if someone still lived there. There were even dirty dishes still on the table.

"Willow, how long did you say Imanie's been dead?"

"About a year now I suppose." She walked over to a chest and opened a drawer and looked through it. There were clothes in it, and she held up one gown after another. "Imanie didn't have any clothes worth wearing. However, she did have some nice jewelry." She closed the drawer and opened another one.

"Why haven't you or your cousins gone through her things by now and cleaned up the place? It doesn't seem as if she has any living relatives to handle it."

"She doesn't. Or at least not that we know of." She slammed closed the drawer and went over and opened a long cupboard that extended from the ceiling to the floor.

Conrad strolled over to the small table in the center of the room and picked up a plate. It had remains of dried food on it yet. "You could have at least cleared the table of the old woman's last meal."

"I suppose we should have. However, once Imanie was buried, none of us wanted to return here. You see, we really had no reason. And now that Fia has married and moved to Scotland, Maira and Morag think it's too sad to spend time here. It was all I could do to convince them to accompany me here the other night."

"Why were you here?"

"I wanted to get this to wear to the festival – the festival that you so rudely dragged me away from." She held up her hand and showed him the bracelet and ring.

"You stole jewelry that didn't belong to you so that you could catch the eye of a nobleman? How honorable of you," he said sarcastically.

She scowled and held her hand over the bracelet, her guilty gaze falling to the ground. "You just said we should have gone through her things. And Imanie doesn't have any living relatives, so what is the problem?"

It thundered again. The sound of raindrops on the roof told Conrad it was time to go.

"What did you need to show me?" he asked. "It's starting to rain, and we need to leave."

"I – I just guess I wanted to visit Imanie's place once more."

"Well, we can come back during the day and when it's not storming." He turned to leave, but her light touch on his arm caused him to stop and look back. "What is it?"

"Do we really have to go so soon?"

"You were the one who wanted to stay at the bonfire. I thought you'd be happy to know we're heading back to the festival."

"But there's no need to hurry anymore. Now that it's raining, the bonfire will be canceled."

"Aye, I suppose it will. Still, if we leave now, we hopefully won't get soaked to the skin."

"Conrad. What was the reason you brought me here in the first place?"

He hesitated to answer. How could he tell her he did it

to get her away from the rest of the noblemen because he was green with envy every time she smiled at them, or they kissed her hand? Thinking of her marrying one of them made him even more determined to win the competitions so he could stop this from happening. He'd made Rook a promise to protect his daughter, and that is what he was doing.

"It's my job to keep you away from the other men," he admitted, not knowing what else to say.

"There's more to it than that, I know there is. I can see it in your eyes."

"Nay, there isn't."

"Why did you join the competition and say you wanted to marry me?"

"I didn't say that." He shifted his weight from one foot to the other and stared at the ground.

"Aye, you did."

"Well, what I meant was –"

He never finished his sentence. Willow stood on her tiptoes and pressed her full lips against his in a sensuous kiss. It was so passionate that when she broke the connection, he almost stumbled backward.

"God's eyes," he said, touching his hand to his mouth. "You have one hell of a kiss, Willow. Why did you do that?"

"I don't know," she said, pulling back a bit. "I suppose I was just trying to use the element of surprise on you."

"I'll say."

"What's the matter, Conrad?" She looked up at him and

batted her thick, black lashes. Her big, brown eyes drew him in. "Didn't you like it?"

Like it? It made him randy, and that was the trouble. He was supposed to be protecting the girl from men and, instead, he wanted nothing more than to throw her down on the bed and make sweet love to her. His mind filled with erotic thoughts that only caused him to harden below his belt. Unfortunately, she noticed.

"I see you did like it after all." She giggled and held her hand to her mouth. Thunder boomed so near and loud that it scared her and made her jump. Her crown fell from her head in the process and landed on the floor. She ended up in his arms clinging to him with her head against his chest. "I'm frightened, Conrad," she told him with a quaver of her voice.

Suddenly, the past all came crashing back into his memories. He felt as if she were that same frightened girl of so many years ago, but now in an adult body. He'd been the one to scare and anger her while growing up. But now it was his duty to protect her from boys who turned into men like him.

"It's all right," he told her in a calming voice, rubbing his hand up and down her back. It was almost as if he felt he needed to make up for all the wrong he did in the past that caused her to hate him. "I'm sorry, Willow."

She looked up in question, still clinging to him as if her life depended on it. "What are you apologizing for?"

"For all the times I teased you when we were children. I never meant to hurt you. What can I do to make up for it?"

Another crash of thunder sounded, followed by the crack of wood and a branch falling from a tree in the secret garden. His horse whinnied. Then he heard the sound of hoofbeats against the damp earth.

"Damn," he cursed, letting go of Willow and running to the entrance. He threw the door open only to see the tail of his horse as it disappeared through the gate of the secret garden. The rain came down in a torrential downpour, already causing deep puddles on the earth. "That last bolt of lightning took down a branch. Between that and the crash of thunder, it spooked the horse. I should have tied her up. I'm going after her."

He had one foot out the door when Willow's words stopped him.

"Kiss me and stay here with me until the storm lets up."

"What did you say?" He turned back to see her picking up her crown from the floor. Her rounded bottom end, the curve of her hips, and her small waist were just too much for a man to bear. She stood up, unintentionally showing him cleavage as she cradled the crown against her bosom.

"You asked me how you could make up for torturing me so many years ago."

"Torture? It wasn't that bad," he answered with a chuckle.

Her eyes opened wide. "I found a snake in my shoe one day, and it almost bit me. I am terrified of snakes. So, if that isn't torture, I don't know what is."

"All right, I suppose I went overboard just a little. But you were so fun to tease." He smiled, thinking of the past.

"And your father never believed it was anyone's fault but yours. That's the funniest part."

"Forget it," she said, slapping her crown on her head and storming to the door. "And don't bother about going after the horse because I'm walking back to the castle."

She was just about out the door when Conrad realized she wasn't jesting. He couldn't let her leave being angry with him. If she walked back in a storm, the earl, not to mention her father, would have his head. Nay, he had to do something to stop her. The only trouble was, she was a determined, headstrong woman who would stop at nothing to get what she wanted. Well, he decided two could play this game.

"You're not going anywhere until the storm lets up." He grabbed her by the wrist and swung her around, pulling her closer to him and kissing her as she had done to him.

She pulled back and slapped him. "I'm not the kind of girl who will forget all about my grievances with just a kiss."

"Then perhaps I need to try a little harder. But I promise you, some way, I'll make you smile before we leave here if it is the last thing I ever do."

He realized she would only fight him, so he did what any man would do in a dire situation. He dipped down, lowering his shoulder. Pulling her over it, he stood back up. Her crown fell from her head in the process. Carrying her, he headed toward the bed.

"Let me down, Conrad," she bit off, hitting his back with her fists and kicking her legs.

"You do realize staring at your bottom end with you wriggling like that is only making me feel randy."

"Put me down, anon," she commanded.

"Stop screaming. It's not becoming of a lady." He flipped her off his shoulder, and she landed on her back on the bed.

"I'll scream if I want to, now get out of my way so I can get off this bed," she warned him.

"If you insist on yelling, I am going to give you something to scream about. And I promise you, it will be from passion and sated desire, not because you want me to leave."

Conrad removed his weapon belt and boots and, in one motion, slipped off his tunic and tossed it across the room.

THE SIGHT of Conrad's muscled chest caused Willow to hold her breath momentarily. He was all man and a very desirable one at that. Nothing about him reminded her any longer of the meddlesome boy she remembered from her past. He gently laid his body atop hers on the bed, making her feel very excited.

Willow stopped fighting Conrad when his mouth covered hers again. His erection pressed up against her through his clothes as he straddled her with one leg. Lost in his kisses, her eyes closed and she felt a fire ignite deep in her belly.

"Willow, you don't know what you're doing to me." His hands caressed her shoulders, slipping down her arms. His kisses trailed to her neck, causing her to throw back her head, giving him access. A tingle of excitement flowed through her. And when his hands cupped her breasts right through her clothes, she gasped in surprise. Her breathing became labored. "You skin is so soft, and your mouth tastes sweet," he mumbled against her neck. "I feel like a bee being drawn in by the essence of a budding, delicate flower." His words sounded romantic, like something written by a bard. But there was one word that came from his mouth that made her a little worried.

"A – a bee?" she asked, suddenly reminded of his stinger when he rubbed up against her leg again. His lips roamed down her neck and toward her cleavage as his hand slowly slid under the hem of her gown and moved up her leg. He suddenly stopped, and his head lifted higher, his hooded eyes looking straight through her.

"You're not wearing a shift or hose?" he asked in a low, sultry voice.

"I d-don't like the feel of them. They make me feel so . . . constricted."

"Bid the devil that makes me wild."

Her heart beat wildly against her ribs, the sound of the drumming in her ears louder than the storm outside. The rain pitter-pattered against the thatched roof almost sounding like music, calming her vivid emotions.

This might be the night she lost her virginity, she realized. The thought intrigued and frightened her at the same time. After all, never in a million years did she think the barrier of her innocence would be broken by someone she imagined she hated all this time. But she didn't hate Conrad anymore. Nay, not really. Now she found herself lusting after him just as he was doing to her.

Right through her gown, he mouthed her nipple, causing it to turn taut. She arched up off the bed, feeling a spiral of heat in her core. She had to have him. She wanted him more than anything she'd ever wanted in her life. Her body called to him and his to her. They were meant to be together, she was sure of it now. Her head fell back as he unlaced her bodice, spreading apart the material and burying his mouth and nose against her bare breasts. His wet lips and tongue suckled and pulled in one of her taut nipples, about sending her squirming off the bed.

"Open for me, Willow." When he pushed up her gown and used his leg to move hers apart, she could no longer hold back her excitement. A moan escaped her lips as she lay with her legs spread and with him in between them. Seeing her bare breasts and Conrad at the same time made her even more excited.

"Hurry," she told him, barely able to stand the feelings inside that threatened to consume her. His hand went to his waist to untie his breeches. That's when it all hit her. They were about to make love, and no one was there to stop them. Why did it feel so good instead of naughty? "I cannot believe I am finally going to know what it's like to make love to a man. My father, nor the earl can stop me now."

"What?" he asked.

For having the power of persuasion and a way with

words, she realized when Conrad stopped abruptly and sat up that she had said the wrong thing. "What are you doing?" she asked, not wanting him to pull away. She was on the brink of release and had to know how it felt.

He dragged a hand through his hair and clenched his jaw. "Damn it," he spat, sliding off the bed.

"Conrad, don't leave me," she called out, but he was already pulling his tunic over his head. It was over now, and she had to do something to keep him from leaving while she was feeling this way. "Come back to bed because I want to feel you inside me. Conrad, I'm ready to burst. Only you can help me find my release. Only you can sate my burning desire."

His hands stilled, and his head snapped upward. She hoped her siren's song would call him back to her.

"Come to me, Conrad. I need you," she begged him.

"Don't even," he ground out, reaching for his weapon belt. "Your words of persuasion aren't going to work on me."

"Why are you getting dressed when we should be making love?"

"I'm doing what I should have done all along instead of being pulled in by your cunning ways. Now get up, we're leaving."

"I am not leaving before I'm finished."

"We're not finishing something we should never have started in the first place."

"Then if you won't help me I'll . . . I'll do it by myself."

"You are jesting." He stopped buckling his weapon belt

and looked up in surprise. "You're a virgin, Willow. I admit it shocked the hell out of me to hear it and I doubt that any other man will believe it either. But no matter how you taunt me, I'll not return to the bed. I made a promise to your father to keep you away from lust-filled men. And instead, I almost deflowered you in a moment of unbridled passion. I'll not continue and neither will you. Now, I won't tell you again. Get off the bed because I'm taking you back to the castle if I have to carry you there in a storm to do it."

"I thought you had changed, but now I see you are still the same as that boy who used to torture me in my youth. You're doing the same thing now."

"I'm doing nothing of the kind."

"I won't forget this, Conrad." She got off the bed and fixed her clothing. Grabbing her crown, she hurried out of the house without looking back.

CONRAD WAITED until Willow left the cottage before he adjusted his breeches, having trouble tying them since he was still aroused. He shook his head as he strapped on his weapon belt. He'd almost believed for a minute that Willow was going to pleasure herself right in front of him. The little tease had made him so hot and bothered that he almost went to her and finished what they'd started. But if he had, it would have been a horrible mistake.

He blew out the flame of the lantern and hurried to the horse, only to find Willow already atop it. Hopefully, the night was dark enough, and she would feel too embarrassed to look below his waist. He took the reins of the horse and headed out of the secret garden.

"Why don't you mount?" she asked him when he started walking the horse through the woods. Her choice of words had him squirming again. Thoughts of mounting her filled his mind. But it wasn't going to happen. He couldn't let it. He'd allowed his emotions and attraction to Willow to get in the way of his job. That was something he could never let happen again.

CHAPTER 10

"*Y*ou did what?" Toby asked Conrad the next morning in his solar. Toby's mouth hung open in surprise.

After returning to the castle last night in the rain, Conrad brought Willow to her chamber and quickly left, locking himself in his own room to ponder the situation. He was glad it rained, and the festival was canceled for the evening. If not, he wasn't sure he would have been able to escort Willow to the rest of the festivities of the night.

"You heard me. I almost made love to Lady Willow last night." He got out of bed, fully dressed, not having bothered to undress before he retired for the evening.

"My lord, excuse me for saying, but do you think Lord Rook would have approved of that?"

"Of course not, you fool!" Conrad poured himself a cup of wine from the decanter on the bedside table and downed it in two gulps. Mayhap he could get drunk enough to forget what happened last night and erase the memory from his mind. "You'll not say a word of this to anyone. Do you understand me?"

"Aye, my lord." Toby still stood there staring at him.

Conrad put down the cup and paced back and forth. "If Lord Rook finds out that, in a moment of passion, I almost took his daughter's innocence, he'll string me up by the neck. Not to mention, he'll no longer honor our deal of being guardian to my sister."

"How – how close did you come?" asked Toby curiously. "And did Lady Willow fight you?"

"We came close enough to scare the hell out of me." He dragged a hand through his hair and walked over to open the shutter. "I never meant for it to go that far. I guess I just wanted to kiss her again, or perhaps scare her so she wouldn't get the idea to go kissing anyone else."

"Was she frightened, my lord?"

"Huh?" He looked over his shoulder, thinking the boy was daft. "She's a temptress and a tease," he told him.

"So . . . she wanted you to bed her?"

"Aye. Nay. Oh hell, I don't know." He continued to pace again.

"What if Lady Willow tells her father what happened?"

He stopped moving, and his spine stiffened. He hadn't thought of that. If she did, everything would be ruined. And then he'd have the wrath of one of the Legendary Bastards of the Crown on his head. That was something he didn't want or need.

"I've got to stop her from telling anyone." He grabbed

for his weapon belt and hurriedly strapped it around his waist.

"Do you think she's already told your sister?" asked Toby, handing Conrad his shoes.

"Hazel," mumbled Conrad looking up with wide eyes. "If she knows what happened, it will frighten her and make her think her own brother is a scoundrel. I've got to get to Willow's room and convince her not to say a word."

He ran to the door in his bare feet, only stopping when Toby called from behind him.

"Your shoes, my lord."

"What's the matter with me?" He hurried back to get his shoes. Lately, he didn't know what made him act the way he did, but when he was around Lady Willow, he couldn't seem to think with a clear head.

* * *

"LADY WILLOW, how was your outing with my brother last night?" Hazel pulled open the shutter, letting the fresh autumn air into the room. Willow welcomed the breeze since she was still feeling hot and bothered from last night. She'd barely slept a wink, tossing and turning all night long. Embarrassed by her behavior, she couldn't believe she actually wanted to give herself to Conrad.

"It was . . . interesting," she said, getting out of bed and reaching for her clothes.

"How so?"

"Your brother isn't what I expected. I'm ashamed to say I almost let him take my innocence."

"What? Conrad seduced you?" Hazel's eyes opened wide.

Before Willow could correct her, the door to the room burst open and Conrad rushed in with one shoe in his hand. His squire was right behind him.

"Conrad!" exclaimed Willow, holding her gown up to hide behind it.

"Willow." Conrad dropped the shoe, and his hand shot up to cover his eyes.

"Turn around, Brother," Hazel instructed, helping Willow to dress quickly.

Willow looked up to see both Conrad and Toby with their backs to her, hiding their eyes with their hands.

"How dare you burst into my room unannounced!" Willow put her hands on her hips. Slowly, Conrad peeked out from between his fingers. Seeing she was dressed, he nudged Toby. They both turned around.

"Willow, can I talk to you in private?" asked Conrad.

"Whatever you have to say, you can do so with witnesses present. After all, I don't want to be alone with you ever again."

"Conrad, how could you have let that happen?" asked Hazel in a low voice.

"God's eyes! Willow told you?" Conrad bent down to get his shoe, hopping on one foot trying to put it on. "Now, Hazel, I don't want you to get the wrong idea of Lady Willow. She was caught up in a moment of passion, but luckily I stopped anything from going too far. I assure you, we didn't do anything – not really."

"I don't think badly about Lady Willow, Brother," said Hazel. "'Tis you I am ashamed of since you seduced her and almost took her virginity." She shook her head. "I never expected you to act that way."

CONRAD SHOOK HIS HEAD, thinking he had heard his sister wrong. Had Hazel just accused him of being the one to initiate the whole ordeal between him and Willow?

"Now, wait a minute, Hazel. I think you must have gotten some wrong information. That isn't at all how it happened."

"Then what did happen?" asked Hazel, watching him intently.

"Aye. I'd like to hear the answer to that, too," said Willow. "Are you insinuating I am a loose woman just because I don't always bind my hair?"

Willow's eyes looked deeply into his, almost as if she could see straight through to his heart. If he wanted Hazel to know the truth, now was the time to tell her that Willow was the one who seduced him and he was the one to pull away. But in doing so, he would ruin Willow's reputation. He cared about her too much to embarrass her like this. If Hazel told anyone else what really happened, Willow's name would be tarnished throughout the castle. Not that it already wasn't, but there would be even more rumors spreading like wildfire that she could possibly be a strumpet. After last night, he realized that wasn't true. After all, she was still a virgin! He knew that now. She was a lady, not a strumpet. He had to make sure no one, not Hazel, Toby, any of the nobles, or even the servants thought any different.

"I'm sorry. I wasn't thinking," he said, holding back the words he really wanted to say. "I let my lust take hold of me. Can you ever forgive me, Lady Willow?"

"Well," she said with a sigh, brushing lint from her sleeve. "I suppose it would be best if all of us kept this to ourselves, don't you agree?"

"I do," said Conrad.

"But Lord Conrad," protested Toby. "I thought you said –"

"Squire, go shine my sword." Conrad yanked his sword from his belt and handed it to Toby. "The hand-to-hand combat starts in an hour, and I want to be sure to look my best when I win."

"Aye, my lord," said Toby heading out the door with the blade in his hand.

"Hazel, are you feeling better?" asked Conrad.

"I am," she said with a nod. "I think I'll go watch the competition with Willow."

"Please do," said Willow, still looking angry. "I want someone with me to witness Sir Conrad losing." She started to pass him on her way to the door, but Conrad grabbed her wrist. She turned back, scowling at him.

"Willow, we need to talk," he whispered.

"I have nothing to say."

"Well, I do. Please, give me a moment alone with you."

She sighed and finally nodded. "Hazel, I forgot my crown and need to get it. Why don't you go down to the practice yard and save me a seat near the front? I'll be there momentarily."

"All right." Hazel stepped up to the doorway. "Aren't you going to escort me, Brother?"

"Toby will do that," said Conrad, calling out Toby's name. His squire hurried back into the room out of breath, with Conrad's sword in his hand.

"Was there something else, my lord?" asked Toby.

"Aye. Take Hazel down to the competition and secure two spots right in the front row for the ladies."

"Of course," he said, escorting Hazel from the room. As soon as they left, Conrad rushed over and closed the door.

"What was that all about?" he asked.

"What was what?" Willow acted as if she really didn't know what he meant. She collected her crown and placed it on her head.

"You know damned well what I'm talking about. You seduced me; it wasn't the other way around."

"I never said you seduced me. That was Hazel who said it." She continued to fuss with her crown.

"I was the one to stop it before we both made a big mistake."

"Mistake?" The hurt in her eyes was evident. "Is that what you call what happened between us? Because it was something special to me."

Now he honestly felt like a cur because he didn't mean it that way. "I didn't mean it was a mistake."

"Then why did you say it?" She batted her long, lush lashes looking so innocent and sweet that it made him want to pull her into his arms again and protect her from men . . . that is, men like him.

"I'm not sure why I used that word."

"Our words are important. We need to choose them wisely, or else someone might misinterpret what we are trying to say."

"Aye, that's true," he told her.

"Yesterday, I might have kissed you to thank you for watching over me, but you were the one to carry me over to the bed, throw me down, and cover me with your body as well as with your kisses."

"I – well, I guess I did do that."

"And I wasn't the one to pull off my clothes. That was you, too. The way I see it, it was a good thing that it didn't go any further. After all, if my father ever heard about this, I would shudder to think what he'd do to you."

"Your father," Conrad mumbled under his breath, envisioning Rook's angry face – three times – as he and his triplet brothers all hunted him down for touching his daughter when Conrad was supposed to be protecting her instead. He supposed he was to blame. A knight never acted that way with a lady. What the hell was the matter with him? "Lady Willow, I beg you to keep this between us and let it go no further."

"I agree," she said, taking his arm. "After all, I would

hate for anything to happen to you. You just need to learn to control your lust, and it'll be fine."

"I will," he said with a nod. "Please excuse my inappropriate behavior and let me escort you to the lists for the competition."

"Thank you, Lord Conrad. And don't give it another thought. Now, let us go to the competition so I can see who might win my hand in marriage."

As Conrad headed to the door with Willow gliding along at his side, he wondered what just happened. He'd entered the room expecting to get an apology from Willow, but he ended up apologizing to her instead. Aye, the wench had a way with words and the power of persuasion. Once again, he fell for her tricks. The odd part was that he was now convinced that the whole thing really was his fault.

CHAPTER 11

W illow watched the competition with Hazel at her side. Each round was hand-to-hand sparring between two competitors. The winner of each round moved on to go up against another competitor until there was one winner in the end.

"My brother is doing quite well," said Hazel. "I hope he wins."

This was the last round. It was down to Conrad and Sir Bedivere. While Willow wanted to see Conrad lose, just to teach him a lesson, she didn't want Sir Bedivere to win. Now that she was being offered as one of the three brides, she didn't want Bedivere to choose her. Sure, she could always say she wouldn't marry him, and the earl would have to honor her wish, but there were only going to be three winners. She didn't want one of the spots to be wasted by the likes of him.

"I hope Conrad wins, too, Hazel," said Willow, reaching out and squeezing the girl's hand for luck.

"You want him to win?" Hazel sounded confused. "If he wins, he might choose to marry you."

"I realize that."

"Then, you want to marry my brother? I don't understand."

Neither did Willow. Before yesterday, she had thought she'd never marry someone like Conrad. But after their intimate time in Imanie's hut, she started to think it wouldn't be so bad. She was attracted to him, and he said he had feelings for her. Envisioning herself married to Conrad was a lot easier than thinking about being Sir Bedivere's wife.

"I never said that." She released Hazel's hand. "I suppose I just don't want Sir Bedivere to win."

"Ah, I understand. He is quite a frightening man."

"What do you mean?" asked Willow curiously.

"He is always staring at me. And yesterday, when I made a trip to the garderobe, he was watching my every move from the corridor outside the great hall."

"What did you do?"

"On the way back to the solar, I took an alternate route so he wouldn't see me. He frightens me, Willow."

"He probably frightens every woman he meets. If he wins, I pity the girl who will be his wife."

"Hello, Lady Willow." Sir George came up and squeezed in between them on the wooden bench.

"Good morning," she said, smiling at him, trying to be

pleasant. Sir George was a baron who had land and money. He wasn't ugly and would be a good catch for any girl to marry. "I'm sorry you didn't win the competition," she told him.

"It's all right. There are still two events to go," he told her. "And when I win, I am going to choose you for my bride."

"You are?" she asked in surprise. Hadn't Conrad told her none of the men would want her for anything but a tryst?

"Of course. Why do you even have to ask?"

"No reason." She looked out, watching Conrad and Bedivere sparring. Bedivere seemed to be getting tired. Conrad had the upper hand. All he had to do was unarm his opponent, and Conrad would win the event. "It's just that Sir Conrad doesn't seem to think anyone will want to choose me as their bride."

"What? You've got to be jesting," said Sir George with a chuckle. "You are the most beautiful of the three." Sir George looked out to the field, put his hands up to his mouth and shouted. "Lochwood, you don't know what you're talking about."

"WHAT?" Conrad looked from the corner of his eye, having heard someone call his name. He'd been in such deep concentration that he hadn't even noticed until now that Sir George was sitting in the lists, so close to Willow that she might as well be on his lap! "What do you mean?" he called back, trying to fight and pay attention to what was happening in the list at the same time. He was only one strike away from unarming Bedivere. But when he looked over his shoulder at Willow, his opponent moved forward, getting the upper hand.

"You said no one would want to marry Lady Willow," Sir George called out, loud enough for everyone to hear. "I assure you, I want her for my wife. I'm going to win and claim her as my bride."

"No, you're not. I am," Bedivere shouted to Sir George, distracting Conrad even more. He didn't like the sound of this. There was no way he was going to let either of the men marry Willow. He had to win this round.

"Look over here, Lochwood," Sir George shouted.

When Conrad glanced back over his shoulder, Sir George had his arm around Willow. He winked at Conrad. That upset him so much that Conrad didn't see the winning blow coming until Bedivere unarmed him.

"The winner is Sir Bedivere of Gaunt!" shouted the announcer. The crowd cheered, and Bedivere held his sword up over his head.

"Tough luck," said the man. "Lady Willow is as good as mine."

That was all Conrad needed to hear. He picked up his sword and gripped it tightly, wanting to fight the knave again. He might have done just that if Earl Alnwick hadn't run out from the stable waving his hands above his head. "It's gone!" he shouted, sounding frantic.

"What's gone? What are you shouting about?" asked Lord Beaufort, rushing out onto the practice field.

"It's my ruby. Someone has stolen my ruby!"

The crowd became restless, and Lord Beaufort had to raise his hand in the air just to be heard. "Don't anyone move!" he called out. "There is a thief among us, and no one will exit my castle walls without being searched."

Conrad looked back over his shoulder. Willow, Hazel, and Sir George were gone.

"THANK YOU FOR THE ESCORT, Sir George, but Lady Hazel and I are going to the garderobe, so there is no need for you to come with us." Willow tried to sound convincing.

"We are?" asked Hazel, not understanding that Willow was trying to get away from the man. Because of Sir George, Conrad had lost the challenge. At one time, this might have made Willow happy, but today it made her sad. She found herself wanting Conrad to win, and he didn't. Now there were only two spots left. If he didn't secure one of them, she would have no chance of marrying him at all.

"Sir George," called out Sir Chester, running across the courtyard to meet them. "Did you hear? Someone has stolen the earl's ruby."

"It's gone?" Willow's heartbeat picked up in pace. That was an expensive stone and very important. Without it, the earl would lose his castle to John of Gaunt, and there would be no chance of making alliances with the Scots. "When did it go missing?" she asked.

"Sometime yesterday, I guess," said Chester. "The crowd is in chaos and everyone is up in arms about this. The earl won't let anyone leave until they are searched. Look, they are closing the gate now. The rest of the competitions are being postponed until the morrow."

The crowd filled the courtyard, being trapped inside the castle walls. People pushed and shoved, and Hazel covered her head and screamed, hunkering down on the ground.

"We've got to get you out of here," said Willow, pulling Hazel to her feet. The girl was frantic and started crying. Willow figured she was frightened of the angry crowd. "Take my hand," she said, grabbing Hazel and pulling her toward the keep. When the guards moved forward in a line with their weapons drawn, Hazel turned pale and looked as if she were about to swoon.

"Willow, I can't breathe," said Hazel, gasping for air.

"Hazel, what is the matter?"

"I feel trapped! I have no air. This happens when I am in small, enclosed places."

People pushed from all sides now, and Willow started feeling faint as well. She spied the stable nearby and knew of only one way to get Hazel out of the crowd and into an open area where she would feel safe.

"We're going for a little ride with the wind in our hair. You will have all the air you need in a few minutes."

"Where are you taking me?" asked Hazel, as Willow

pulled her into the stable, yanking open the stall gate, and quickly throwing a bridle on her mare.

"We are going somewhere where we will stay until the frenzied crowd calms down."

"But you heard what Sir Chester said." Hazel tried to catch her breath and held a hand to her chest. "They are searching everyone. They won't let us leave."

"They won't be able to stop us." She pushed a bench over to the horse and nodded. "Now get on the horse."

"But it isn't saddled."

"We don't need a saddle. We'll ride together and leave through the hidden postern gate. We'll stay in the secret garden until the earl opens the gates and the crowd dissipates."

"Aye, I like the garden," said Hazel, calming down at the thought. "Willow, please don't leave me. I don't want to be alone. I'm frightened."

"There's nothing to fear. I'm sure Lord Beaufort will find the thief. We are safe." She mounted behind Hazel and took the reins. "Now hold on because as soon as we go through the postern gate, we're going to ride fast. I don't want your brother seeing us and confining us to our chamber again."

"Nay, we don't want that," said Hazel with a shake of her head. "Thank you, Willow. I've never had a true friend before. I feel as if you are my friend to risk being caught and punished just to help me."

"I feel that you are a friend, too, Hazel." Willow said the words to calm the girl, but it wasn't the only reason. In her heart, she wanted to help Hazel because she had started to care for the girl. And in these past few days, she felt she'd made a new friend, too.

* * *

"WHAT DO you mean you don't know where Lady Hazel and Lady Willow are?" growled Conrad, pushing his way through the frenzied crowd in the courtyard while the guards searched one person after another looking for the ruby.

"I was with you, my lord. I didn't know it was my job to watch over the women. I was attending you during the competition like any good squire would do for his lord."

"You're right, Toby. I didn't mean to lose my temper. But watching over Lady Willow is proving to be a challenge. Mayhap I should pull out of the competition."

"Aye, please do," said Sir Bedivere, breaking through the crowd with a ribbon in his hand for winning the sword event. "That would be best since you can't seem to keep track of a simple wench. Once Lady Willow is my wife, she won't go anywhere unless she is right at my side. I will tie her to me if I have to, but she won't be off batting her eyes and smiling at other men, I assure you of that."

"She is not a hound, Bedivere. And if you think I'll pull out of the competition so you can have her, you've got another guess coming."

"Face it. She doesn't want you, Lochwood. If she did, she wouldn't keep running from you, would she?"

Something about the man's words hit Conrad hard. Willow did seem to keep avoiding him, even more so since their intimate moments last night.

"Let's go, Toby," said Conrad, plowing through the crowd, stretching his neck, looking for the girls. He felt as if he were failing miserably as guardian to Willow. He also felt as if he'd not seen much of his sister in days. Hazel had times when she became very frightened or extremely sad. She needed constant supervision. Once she went to live at Naward Castle with Lord Rook, she would have it. But for now, he needed to keep a closer eye on her. He'd been so preoccupied with Willow that his sister's care had fallen at the wayside. He wasn't happy about this at all.

"They've got to be here somewhere," said Toby, looking in all directions. People shouted, and others pushed. Dogs barked, and little children cried. It all made Conrad's head hurt.

"Check their solar, Toby. If they are there, stand post outside their door until I return."

"Where are you going, my lord?"

"If they were in this commotion, Hazel probably started acting odd again."

"Odd? How so?"

"It doesn't matter, Squire. Check the chamber, but if I know Willow, that is the last place she'd go."

"Then where do you think they went?"

"There's only one place I can think of that is calm and serene. After last night, I doubted Willow would ever return there, but something tells me she took my sister to the secret garden."

"You're saying they left the castle walls? But the gate is closed. No one is being let out."

"A simple gate cannot stop a determined, cunning woman like Willow. If she wants something, she will get it one way or another. And I am willing to bet, this is one of those times."

CHAPTER 12

As soon as they got through the hidden postern gate and on the trail in the woods leading to the secret garden, Hazel stopped trembling. That told Willow she did the right thing by taking the girl away from the chaos at the castle. She didn't like to see Hazel suffer like this. It wasn't right.

"Mayhap, we can stay here for a little while, and you will feel better." Willow hopped off the horse and helped Hazel to dismount. She made sure to tie the reins of the horse to a tree so it wouldn't run off like it did when she was here with Conrad.

Conrad. Just looking toward the cottage, she felt her heart break. She had never been turned down by a man before and didn't know how to react to what happened. Then again, she'd never gotten so close to making love before either. Lost in her thoughts, she wasn't paying attention to Hazel. When she looked back, the girl was bent over pulling weeds again.

"What are you doing?" asked Willow. "We are here so you can calm down and relax. We're not here for you to work like a servant."

"But I enjoy gardening," Hazel told her, sounding as if she meant it. "By working with the earth, it helps me to forget my troubles."

"Oh, I see," said Willow, not sure she understood it at all. When Willow wanted to relax, she took a hot bath or sipped on spiced mead lounging in the orchard. But seeing the smile on Hazel's face, she decided to let the girl do what she wanted.

"If you really want to pull some weeds, you can clear out the bramble by Imanie's grave. It is so overgrown, I can barely see the wooden cross that my cousins and I placed there."

"I could?" Hazel looked up with wide eyes and held her hand to her heart. "I would be honored."

"I'm sure Imanie would be honored as well. Wherever she is." Willow yawned and stretched, looking back at the cottage, wanting to get out of the sun.

"You seem tired, Willow." Hazel kept her head down as she weeded a trail toward Imanie's final resting place.

"I didn't sleep very well last night," she admitted, wanting nothing more than a few minutes to close her eyes.

"Why don't you go into the cottage and lie down for a while?" suggested Hazel.

"I don't know." Willow felt apprehensive about leaving the girl alone. Hazel had some apparent fears and problems, and Willow wasn't sure what the girl was capable of doing.

"I won't be going anywhere if that is what worries you." Hazel smiled and wiped the back of her hand against her cheek, leaving a smudge of dirt. "There is so much to be done here, that I could stay here for a month and never leave. It makes me happy."

"An hour or two is all we have for today, but mayhap I can convince Conrad to let you come here for a short while every day."

"Oh, would you?" Hazel's eyes lit up and sparkled in the sun. "I would like that, Willow. Thank you for being my friend."

"Of course," she said, making her way up the stairs. "Just call out if you need me. I'm going to close my eyes for only a few minutes."

Willow entered the house and stopped in her tracks when she noticed the rumpled bedcovers, knowing what made them that way. Visions of Conrad's naked chest lodged in her mind, as well as the feeling of heat spiraling through her as he kissed her in the most intimate places. Her body vibrated for him, but she realized that what they almost did was not the way a proper lady acted. She had lost control. That was something that had never happened before when it came to men. Always being careful to pull them in with interest and then back away before anything happened, she wondered why she had no willpower to stop when she was with Conrad.

Strolling over to the bed, she sat down, running her hand along the covers. Then she laid down and buried her nose in the pillow. His scent of pine and leather filled her senses, making her want to cry because she could not have him. It was wrong, she told herself, closing her eyes, squeezing them shut and feeling the tears trapped beneath her lids.

"Why didn't he want me?" she murmured to herself, never feeling so empty and rejected in all her life. Without meaning to, she drifted off to sleep, finding herself in the presence of her late mentor again.

"Willow, what are you doing?" came Imanie's scolding voice.

In her sleep, she sat up, seeing the old woman standing at the foot of the bed.

"Imanie. You're here," she said, trying to figure out why the woman had come to her again from the grave.

"Of course, I'm here. This is my home. And now that you're here, I want to know what you're going to do about it."

"About what?" she asked, thinking at first that she was talking about her tryst with Conrad. Imanie clucked her tongue and shook a scolding finger.

"I'm not talking about him," she said as if she'd read Willow's mind. "And where that is concerned, you need to stop tempting him like that. It is not becoming of a lady."

"I didn't tempt him."

"Didn't you, now?" Imanie raised an eyebrow the way she always used to do when she knew Willow was lying.

"Oh, all right, so I did. But I really wanted to make love to him, so it wasn't just teasing him like he claims it was."

"Men don't have the control that women do when it comes to the bedchamber. Of course, from what I witnessed, you don't have it either."

"Witnessed?" Willow held her hand to her bodice, clutching it tightly to her. "You were watching us?"

"I'm a spirit, Willow. I can go anywhere and see anything, and don't you forget it. What is going to happen to Conrad when your father gets home and finds out what happened?"

"What do you mean? He won't find out."

"Who all knows about it?" the old woman asked.

"Just Conrad and me."

"That's all?"

She thought about it for a moment and shook her head. "And Hazel. And Conrad's squire, Toby, as well."

"Men aren't good at keeping secrets. Even if it's not intentional, you need to realize Toby will probably let the secret out."

"What can I do about it, Imanie? How can I keep Conrad from being punished by my father? It wasn't his fault."

"That's not what Hazel thinks. And you did nothing to correct her."

"Oh, Imanie, I wasn't thinking. I need to figure out something to help Conrad. My father can never know."

"The only thing that could stop that from happening is if you were married to the man. Then it wouldn't matter."

"Marry Conrad?" The mere thought made her heart flutter faster.

"You like him and have feelings for him, don't you?"

"Why, yes. However, I don't think he feels the same way about me. After all, he left me on the edge of release when I needed him the most."

"And don't you think that hurt him even more than it did you?"

"Then why did he pull away so abruptly?"

"Don't be daft, Willow. He did it to save your name and reputation. What would happen if he'd taken your virginity and then you were betrothed to someone else? No man is stupid enough not to know that his wife isn't a virgin on her wedding night."

"Imanie, I feel so horrible about what happened. I wasn't thinking. I need to make it up to Conrad."

"That's fine, but what you should really be thinking about right now is finding the thief who stole the ruby."

"The earl's ruby? Why me?"

"Willow, did I teach you nothing? You have been chosen by the late queen to be a Follower of the Secret Hearts. You need to prove to the others in the group, as well as to yourself, that Philippa didn't make a mistake by putting you in this position."

"Nay, she didn't make a mistake." Willow touched the golden heart brooch pinned to her gown. She never went anywhere without wearing it. Perhaps she wasn't doing what her late queen would have wanted her to do. Willow needed to be more like Fia, and do something to help someone as well. "What can I do?" asked Willow.

"You can stop thinking so much about yourself and, instead, help Earl Alnwick find that ruby. If he doesn't have the ruby to give to the king, he is going to lose his castle. Do you think John of Gaunt will try to make alliances with the Scots, the way the earl wants to do?"

"Nay, I don't. Getting that ruby to the king is essential. The fate of two nations might depend on it. Mayhap I can talk to my cousin, Richard, and convince him to let the earl keep his castle."

"Do you really believe Richard would do that if there was nothing in it for him?"

Imanie's question hit her hard. Willow suddenly felt as if she'd been selfish, and was no better than her greedy cousin. There was so much more at stake here. "Nay," said Willow. "Richard will not help him without the ruby in trade. I promise I will use any means possible and find the gemstone and help the earl. I am a Follower of the Secret Hearts and just as strong as Fia."

"Then prove it, Willow, because everyone thinks you are a spoiled girl who believes she is better than anyone else and only thinks of herself."

"That's not true."

"Hazel is pulling weeds. Why don't you prove that statement to yourself and go help her."

The thought of getting down in the dirt and pulling weeds horrified Willow. "I am a noble," she cried. "I wasn't meant to do manual labor."

"Hazel is a noble as well, but yet you see how happy it makes her doing something to beautify the earth. She doesn't feel it is beneath her to do such a task."

"But Hazel is different. She's . . . odd."

"Mayhap, there is something you can learn from the girl.

Now stop judging her and start changing or Sir Conrad will never want you for his wife."

"Imanie, wait," she said, sitting up in bed, looking around the room, sure the vision was real. Through the open door, she saw Hazel on her hands and knees at Imanie's grave. A pile of weeds grew higher and higher at her side. Hazel reached up and wiped her brow, never letting her concentration leave the task she was committed to doing.

Willow got out of bed and walked over to the door, holding on to the doorjamb as she struggled with her decision. Part of her wanted to help Hazel, but another part of her felt disgusted, knowing this was not the work of a noblewoman.

Then Imanie's last words made her reconsider. The woman was right. If Conrad thought she was naught but spoiled, he would never want her for his wife. And not only that, but she needed to figure out a way to find the ruby or the fate of two nations might be doomed.

"I have work to do," she said aloud, reaching to her shoulder to remove her attached tippets. The sleeves of a noblewoman's gown were detachable so they wouldn't get dirty. And if a dress started to look worn, the sleeves could be added to a new gown altogether. Willow had never rooted around in the mud like a pig before. She wasn't sure what was going to happen once she started pulling weeds, but she was about to find out.

* * *

CONRAD RODE through the gate of the secret garden, squinting in the sun, not sure what was going on. Willow's horse was tethered to a nearby tree, and he thought he heard laughing and singing coming from behind a big pile of weeds. He slipped off his horse and tied it to the tree, keeping his eyes focused across the garden. A crooked path cleared of weeds led across the yard. He followed it, approaching slowly, recognizing his sister's voice as well as Willow's singing a cheery song he had never heard before.

He walked up to the pile of weeds almost as tall as him, peeking around it curiously. "Hello?" Conrad stepped out into the open to find both Hazel and Willow sitting on the ground in the dirt.

"Conrad," exclaimed Willow, jumping to her feet with weeds in her grasp. Her hair was disheveled, and dirt streaked her face. If he wasn't mistaken, he swore he saw a bead of perspiration on her brow. Her gown was filthy. Her crown sat atop a nearby rock. But the oddest part that made him laugh was the fact that Willow had removed the tippets of her dress and had bare arms up to her shoulders since she didn't wear a chemise beneath her gown.

"Brother, how nice to see you," said Hazel from the ground. She reached out and brushed away dirt from a ring of rocks that outlined Imanie's grave. "How do you like what we did? Now, we'll always know where poor, old Imanie is buried, no matter how high the weeds get."

"Willow?" Conrad wondered if the girl had gone mad. "What are you doing on the ground in the dirt? And without your sleeves?"

"I'm helping your sister pull weeds." She held up a handful of weeds and dropped them atop the pile.

"I can see that." He walked around her, eying her up and down. This didn't seem like the same girl he knew. "I heard you both singing and laughing when I walked up. Have you been drinking wine or, perhaps, whisky?"

"Conrad, how can you say such a thing?" asked Hazel. "We were just having fun."

"Fun," Conrad repeated, nodding and trying to comprehend what was going on here. He was sure Willow had never dug in the dirt in her life and wouldn't be caught dead doing what she considered was the work of servants. He expected this odd behavior from his sister, but not from Willow. He didn't understand it.

"You should try it, said Willow with a smile. "Hazel said gardening helps her to relax and forget about her problems. It makes her happy and calm. I didn't believe it until I tried it for myself. It really does work." She scratched the side of her face, leaving a long streak of dirt in its place.

"You two never should have left the castle. Come on, Hazel, we're going back." He pulled his sister to a standing position and noticed the smile disappear from her face.

"But I'm not finished yet. Just look at all the weeds that need to be pulled. And after that, I want to trim the bushes and thin out some of the lilies. I was thinking of even planting a few radishes since they grow fast and will thrive in the approaching cold weather."

"Hazel, brush off your clothes and meet us by the

horses. Willow, I'd like a word with you in the house please."

"Of course," said Willow, picking up her crown and placing it on her head cockeyed. He followed her inside the cottage where she picked up her tippets and started to button them back on. "This is difficult to do by myself. Would you mind helping me?"

"Willow," he said, taking one of her sleeves and securing it as he spoke. "Why did you come here with Hazel?"

"She was very upset when the crowds starting pushing and yelling. She was crying, and I thought she was about to pass out. Did you know her body was trembling until we got away from everyone and were halfway to the secret garden?"

"Hazel has a lot of fears. That is why I am securing a place at your father's castle for her. I don't know how to help her. I think being around your mother will be good for her."

"You're pushing her away when you should be pulling her closer. You are all she has, Conrad. She is still very upset about the death of your parents, especially your mother."

"And so am I," he told her. "Hazel is frail and not at all well. You should never have brought her here. She needs to stay in her chamber and be monitored at all times. I'm afraid I have been too lenient with her and now look what's happened."

"But all she needs is to be noticed, Conrad. Not locked away and hidden as if she were addled."

"Willow, you don't understand. Hazel needs help, and I don't have the time to give her the care she needs. I have not only a castle to run, but also a small army at my command waiting for me to return to Scarborough. Once I have a wife, things will be different. But for now, I need her to go with your father to live at Naward. And if your father changes his mind, then I will have no choice but to put her in a convent for her own safekeeping. At least there, I will know she is safe and being watched over at all times."

"Nay! I don't want to go to a convent. And neither do I want to live in Naward," came Hazel's voice from the door.

"Hazel," said Conrad in surprise. "How long have you been standing there?"

"Long enough to hear that I'm naught but a thorn in your side and that you can't wait to get rid of me." Crying, the girl ran across the garden toward the horses.

"What is the matter with you?" yelled Willow, yanking the other sleeve from Conrad's hand. "All the poor girl wants is your attention – anyone's attention, and you want to hide her away like she's a leper or something."

"That's not true, now calm down. I only want to help her."

"If that's the truth, then make her feel special. Show her you care about her and stop pushing her away as if you are embarrassed that she is your sister."

"Willow," he said under his breath, wetting his lips. This was a very uncomfortable situation. "You don't under-stand. Hazel isn't like you or me or anyone else. She has certain . . . problems. There are things that I don't even understand. You have no idea."

"Well, I would like to know her better and wish you would try to get closer to her as well."

Conrad groaned and wiped his hand over his face. He didn't have time for this. "I don't want to talk about this right now. And I don't want you bringing my sister here to sit in the dirt again. Do you understand?"

"Oh, I understand all right. If someone doesn't act the way you want them to, then you push them away and try to forget anything ever happened at all."

"You're not talking about Hazel anymore, are you? You are talking about what happened to us in this very room."

"You can't keep pushing away the people who care about you, because if you don't stop it, you are going to end up with no one."

"This is nonsense. I don't push people away. Now, I won't hear another word. The earl's ruby has been stolen. We need to get back to the castle anon. There is a thief out there somewhere, and there is no telling how dangerous he is. I don't want you or Hazel going off on your own again."

"Don't worry about the thief, I am going to catch him and make sure the ruby is returned to the earl."

"Stop talking nonsense."

"Nonsense, is it? Perhaps, you don't think I'm capable of doing such a thing?"

"I don't know, and neither do I want to. Now, get to your horse and –"

He stopped in midsentence when he heard the sound of

hoofbeats leaving the garden. "Damn," he spat, running to the door. "Hazel just left. I need to catch her before she does something stupid."

"There you go again. Now you are calling your sister stupid."

"We'll talk about this later. I have to catch up to her." He ran for the horse with Willow right on his heels. He mounted and was about to leave when he realized Willow was stranded there. "Give me your hand," he said, leaning over and reaching out for her.

"Nay." She clutched the tippets and backed away. "I'm not going to ride with you."

"It's that, or you'll stay here by yourself since we've only got the one horse now. So, give me your hand and hurry up about it."

She stubbornly resisted. "I'll stay here by myself, I don't care. But I'm not riding with you."

"Woman, you try my patience!" Conrad reached down and grabbed her under the arms, lifting her up and plopping her down in front of him atop the horse.

"Careful!" she cried out. "I almost lost my crown." Her hand went to her crown to secure it. "If you think I'm riding into the castle without my sleeves and with dirt streaked across my face, then you've got another guess coming."

Conrad turned the horse and headed out of the secret garden, holding his arm around Willow's waist even though she struggled and dug her fingers into his arm trying to get loose.

"Aye, that's the Willow I know. I wondered where she went." Holding her close so she wouldn't fall, he directed his horse into a run to catch up with his sister. Once again, being Willow's guardian was proving to be exhausting, and he didn't know how much longer he could keep this up.

CHAPTER 13

"Where were you last night, Lochwood?" asked Sir Chester the next morning, as he and Sir George met Conrad in the corridor just outside Willow's room. Conrad's squire was nowhere to be found. Because of it, Conrad overslept. He hoped Willow and Hazel were ready because he was starved and didn't want to miss the first meal of the day.

"I retired early," he told them, not wanting the man to know he'd snuck back in the hidden postern gate with Willow and Hazel after dark. The search for the ruby was still going on, and no one had noticed them entering the keep and heading to their chambers. He would have returned the way he'd left through the front gate since he'd already been searched, but Willow insisted she would just die if any of the noblemen saw her without her sleeves and with dirt on her face and gown. She had wanted to stop at the creek to wash up but, after finding

Hazel, he didn't want to chance it that the girls would run off again.

Neither of the women was talking to him now since they were so angry with him. If he was lucky, mayhap they'd cooled down and would speak to him this morning when he escorted them to the great hall for the morning meal.

He still didn't understand why Willow had been acting so strange yesterday but planned on having a good, long conversation with her about it today.

"I didn't see Lady Willow around here either last night," said Sir George.

"My sister was upset by the turn of events and the chaotic crowd," explained Conrad. "Willow took her to their chamber early."

"That's funny," said Chester. "One of the guards came to their room with a handmaiden to search them, and there was nobody there."

"For God's sake, what is going on?" spat Conrad. "They are ladies, not thieves. I will talk to Lord Beaufort about this personally."

"It was his idea," said Sir George, leaving Conrad at a loss for words.

The door to Willow's chamber sprang open. Willow emerged with Hazel standing silently right behind her. Willow was dressed to the hilt, looking like a queen. Gone were the smears of dirt on her face and the soiled gown. Her hair was actually braided this morning and tucked under the crown on her head. With her low-cut bodice, she boldly displayed much more cleavage than she should. That damned gold heart brooch she always wore winked at him in the light, drawing even more attention to her chest.

"There you are," said Willow, sounding happy and like she was no longer angry with him. "I was starting to wonder if you'd gotten the squire's message."

"What message?" asked Conrad. "I can't even find Toby. Did you send him somewhere?"

"We're ready to go if you are," Willow continued. Hazel nodded silently in agreement from behind her.

"Ladies, shall we?" Conrad held out his arm and stepped forward, but Willow reached out and took Sir Chester's arm instead. Hazel shyly took the arm of Sir George."

"What is going on here?" growled Conrad. "I don't know what kind of game you're playing, but I don't like it."

"Oh, Sir Conrad. I didn't even see you there," said Willow, making both of the other knights chuckle. "If you'll excuse us, we don't want to be late for the feast."

"Wait," he said, stopping the barons in their tracks. "The Ladies Willow and Hazel are my responsibility. I will escort them to the great hall."

"Then why did your squire come to our solar this morning and ask us to take the ladies there?" asked Sir George.

"He did?" Conrad's brows dipped. "I didn't send him with any message."

"I did," stated Willow boldly. Her hand went to straighten her crown as she spoke. "After all, Lady Hazel and I don't want to be escorted by anyone who doesn't want us near them."

"Stop it," said Conrad. "This isn't funny, Willow."

"I want you near me, Lady Willow," said Chester, putting his hand over hers atop his arm and smiling from ear to ear. Conrad didn't miss the man's glance down at Willow's cleavage. His blood boiled. He felt as if he wanted to kill the man or strangle Willow, or perhaps both.

"Good day, Sir Conrad," said Willow, laughing and talking with the knights as the four of them headed to the great hall. Conrad stood there with his mouth open, unable to believe that not only Willow but also his sister had just disobeyed him.

"Ah, there you are, my lord," said Toby, hurrying down the corridor, looking over his shoulder at the foursome as he walked. "Why are the barons escorting the ladies?"

"Where the hell have you been, Squire?"

"Well, after Lady Willow came to the door this morning and asked me to deliver a missive to Sir Chester and Sir George, she had me deliver a missive to Lord Beaufort as well. I am just now returning."

"What are you talking about? No one came to my door this morning."

"Aye, she did," insisted Toby. "You slept right through it, my lord. Your snoring was so loud I could barely hear Lady Willow since she was whispering. I was going to wake you, but she said I should let you sleep."

"Since when do you take orders from her? What is the matter with you?"

Toby shrugged his shoulders. "I'm not sure why I did it. I suppose it was because she asked so sweetly and it sounded important. She told me you wouldn't mind."

"You fool. Don't you realize what you did?"

"I only delivered missives."

"Aye, missives asking the knights to escort the ladies to the great hall this morning. And I'm sure the message to Lord Beaufort was asking him to seat them all together at the dais."

"Ooooh, I see," said Toby. "Sorry about that, my lord. But mayhap, Willow's reason for doing this was because you said neither of them was talking to you, being so angry with you and all."

"Thank you for pointing that out. From now on, if you do anything, and I mean anything at all for Lady Willow without my knowledge of it first, I will have you flayed. Do you understand?"

"Aye, my lord. Are you going to go down to the great hall and demand they let you escort them instead?"

The thought crossed his mind. Actually, he also had ideas about throwing a few good punches at Sir Chester, and then Sir George and then Sir Chester again. But he wouldn't. Instead, he needed to figure out just what Willow was doing.

"Nay," said Conrad. "I am going to let the girls stew in the trouble they are brewing. They'll come running back to me when Sir George and Sir Chester frighten them."

"What if they don't?" asked Toby. "What if the ladies

enjoy being with the barons more than they like being with you?"

That made Conrad think. Hadn't Willow said something about him not wanting them, and now they were with the barons? What had he done? His sister was hurt and angry overhearing what he said about her, and Willow was acting so odd he didn't know what she was thinking. Willow made the comment that she was going to find the thief and get the ruby returned to Earl Alnwick. He was curious how she thought she was going to accomplish that task. Mayhap, he'd sit back and just watch for a while as things unfolded. He'd watch from a distance, but still stay close enough to step in at the first sign of trouble.

"Toby, I don't know what Lady Willow is up to, but I can guarantee you whatever it is, it's dangerous, stupid, ridiculous, and I'm not going to like it."

"Shall we stop her?" asked Toby.

"Nay," answered Conrad. "Lady Willow is sly and cunning, but she is also naïve. That is what scares me."

"Do you think the knights will try to take advantage of her?"

"They try anything, and mark my words, I will step in and stop it before it begins. The last thing I want is for anything to happen to either of the two women who mean something to me."

"I've never heard you talk this way before," said Toby.

"That's because I've never met anyone like Lady Willow before, and I doubt I ever want to again."

* * *

WILLOW'S PLAN was working beautifully. She not only managed to make Conrad jealous, but she also secured a spot next to Sir Chester during the meal. This was her time to question him and find out if he could possibly be the one who stole the earl's ruby.

"Lady Willow, we were surprised to get your missive this morning," said Chester.

"Aye," agreed Sir George from next to him. "It's such a pleasure to escort you ladies to the dais table."

"We appreciate it, don't we Lady Hazel?" Willow asked, trying to pull the shy girl into the conversation.

"We do," said Hazel.

Willow saw Conrad enter the great hall with his squire. All the seats at the dais were taken since Willow brought the barons, so there was nowhere for Conrad to sit. He said something to his squire and then walked straight up to the dais. Willow sat next to Sir Chester on one side, and Lord Beaufort's wife, Lady Ernestine, on the other. Earl Alnwick was on the other side of Lord Beaufort.

"Good morning, Earls," said Conrad approaching the raised table.

"Lochwood, it seems your spot has been taken," said Beaufort. "Perhaps, we can make room for you at the table if we all squeeze in."

"No need." Conrad raised a hand. "Everyone seems quite comfortable. I wouldn't want to upset that." His eyes flashed over to Willow. She quickly looked the other way. "Did you find the thief who stole the ruby?" asked Conrad.

"Nay, not yet," answered Earl Alnwick. "But I'm not giving up hope."

"That's right," said Beaufort. "Everyone who hasn't been searched yet will be searched today before the competition continues."

"As they should," agreed Conrad.

"Lady Willow, I don't believe you have been searched yet. Nor Lochwood's sister," said Lord Beaufort.

"Me?" Willow looked up in surprise. "Lord Beaufort, surely you don't think I had anything to do with the disappearance of the ruby?" She picked up the goblet and took a sip of wine.

"I can search her for you," said Conrad, almost causing her to choke on the wine when she heard him. She coughed, and Sir Chester patted her on the back.

"I'm sure Lady Willow and Lady Hazel don't really need to be searched," said Lord Beaufort's wife. "After all, they are nobles and Willow is your ward, Walter."

"Nay, I insist we be searched just like everyone else," said Willow. "Shall we do it now, so wagging tongues don't start rumors?" Willow stood up, and Sir Chester jumped to his feet as well.

"Sit down, Willow," said Conrad under his breath. "No one thinks you're a thief. Now, eat your meal."

"I'm no longer hungry," Willow retorted, not liking the fact Conrad was telling her what to do. "Sir Chester, if you don't mind, will you escort me back to my chamber?"

"Me, too," said Hazel, jumping up as well, followed by Sir George.

"Now, now, I don't want my meal interrupted," said Beaufort. "I'm sure it can wait."

"Conrad, I'm not feeling well," said Hazel. "Will you walk me back to the room?"

"I'll do it," said Sir George, putting his hand on her shoulder.

"I'm her brother. She'll feel more comfortable with me." Conrad climbed the dais to help his sister. "Willow, are you coming?"

"Me?" Willow saw this as an opportunity and didn't want to waste it. If Conrad was with Hazel, she could be alone with Sir Chester and try to figure out if he was the thief. "I haven't eaten yet."

"You just said you weren't hungry," Conrad reminded her.

"Well, I've changed my mind." She sat back down.

"Fine. I'll be back for you."

As soon as they left the room, Willow sprang into action. "Sir Chester, would you like to go for a stroll?"

Chester was just spooning some stewed rabbit onto his trencher, and his hand stopped. "Now? But the food is just being served." He looked like a man who liked to eat, so she was sure he wouldn't want to miss a meal.

She had to convince him to go with her now. If she waited until the meal ended, Conrad would be back and be watching her like a hawk. It was her duty to her late queen and her country to use her skills to find out the answers she needed. Boldly, she placed her hand on his arm and looked deeply into his eyes. "I thought you wanted to get to know me before the competitions are over."

"There will be plenty of time for that after the meal," said Sir Chester, taking a bite of the stew and making a slight moan of delight.

"I'll go with you, Lady Willow," said Sir George, now sitting by himself since Hazel had left.

"I'd like that very much."

Sir George got up, but Sir Chester jumped to his feet as well. "Nay, I'm taking her."

"I'd like to get to know both of you," she told them. "Perhaps all three of us could go for a stroll?"

The men chuckled.

"I've never strolled with three before," said Sir George.

"Neither have I, but I'm willing to try it," added Sir Chester.

"Great! We can make it a threesome," said Willow, noticing the lustful looks on the men's faces. "I mean, a walk with all of us," she corrected herself. Taking hold of one man's arm on each side of her, she strolled across the great hall and out the door. They were about to take her outside, but in order to know if they had the ruby, she would have to search through their things in their solar.

"Where would you like to go, Lady Willow?" asked Sir George.

"The two of you are sharing a solar, aren't you?" she asked.

"We are." Sir Chester exchanged a glance with Sir George.

"Why don't we go there and have a glass of wine?" asked Willow.

"I like that idea." Sir George took a decanter of wine and a goblet off the tray of a passing server. "Now we're set." He chuckled. It made Willow's stomach turn into a knot. Mayhap she was playing with fire as Conrad had told her. The last thing she wanted to do was to get burned.

"Our solar is just down the corridor," said Sir Chester.

As they walked, Willow started up with the questions. "A ruby the size of the one that the earl had stolen must be worth a lot."

"Aye, it is." Sir George poured wine into the goblet as he walked.

"I'll bet anyone would give just about anything to have it."

"I know I would," said Chester with a chuckle.

"It would pay off a lot of my debts," added George.

"I remember when I heard it was stolen, I was standing in the courtyard talking," said Willow. "I was astounded. I'll bet both of you were torn away from your own activities when you heard the announcement as well."

"Aye, I was waiting for Sir Bedivere in the great hall, but he never showed up," Sir George told her. "It seems he was waiting at the mews for me instead, talking with the Ladies Anabel and Grace."

"I was in the practice yard preparing for the competition," said Sir Chester.

"I wonder what the guard who was watching the ruby was doing when it was stolen?" asked Willow.

"Mayhap, you should ask Lord Bedivere," commented Chester under his breath.

"Aye, he has seemed to befriend the guard. I heard he'd been asking to see the ruby again several times after our initial viewing," added Sir George.

Willow didn't think either of these men stole the ruby, but she still needed to be sure. She wanted to go through their trunks in their room to see if she could possibly find it hidden there.

"Here we are, my lady." Sir Chester opened the door to the solar. Willow's heart raced. It wasn't proper to enter the room with the men. If anyone saw her, they might get the wrong idea. There could be an entire scandal. Still, she felt it was her duty as a member of the Followers of the Secret Heart to investigate further.

Looking over her shoulder, she scanned the corridor, glad she didn't see anyone watching. All she had to do was to make up an excuse to get the men to leave, and she could go through the room quickly and search it before they returned. Since Lord Beaufort had already searched them, if one of them were the thief, they would have probably hidden the ruby back in their things afterward. She had to know.

"Lady Willow, how about some wine?" asked Sir George holding up the goblet and decanter and smiling.

"Oh, yes. Of course. Just put it on the table. I will have some in a minute. I think I'd like a breath of fresh air."

Willow hurried to the window and threw open the shutter. If the men tried anything with her, she could always yell out the window for help.

"Come, sit on the bed and talk with us," said Sir George, plopping down on the pallet and patting the area next to him.

"Aye, we would like to get to know you," added Sir Chester. "After all, if we win one of the last two competitions, you might be the wife of one of us."

That thought didn't sit well with Willow. Not that the barons weren't kind, but she couldn't picture being married to either of them. She tried to push the vision from her head because she could only see being married to Conrad.

She decided she needed to find out her information and leave quickly. Conrad was sure to go back to the great hall and notice she was missing. Willow didn't want him to know she was here. He would only think she was leading the men on and playing a game again. Sadness filled her heart as she realized that was exactly what she was doing. Even though she had a purpose behind it, Conrad wouldn't care.

She walked over and purposely knocked over the decanter of wine and the goblet. They fell to the floor, spilling wine everywhere.

"Oh, my!" She pretended it was an accident. "I am so careless. How will we have our wine now?"

"I'll get some more wine. I'll be right back." Sir Chester ran to the door and left the room. One down, and one more to go. However, Sir George was still sitting on the bed smiling at her and looking more than comfortable.

"Silly me," said Willow, faking a laugh. "I forgot to tell Sir Chester I prefer red wine over white. White wine sours my stomach." She held her stomach for effect.

"I'll tell him," said George jumping up and hurrying to the door. "Stay here, I will be right back."

As soon as the door closed, Willow ran to the corner and threw open a trunk and started digging through their belongings, hoping to find the ruby. In one trunk she was surprised to find needlepoint! She held up a cloth embroidered with colorful flowers, noticing Sir George's initials on the bottom. She might have thought a lady had given it to him, but when she found more needlepoint that was in progress at the bottom of the trunk, she realized she had discovered an embarrassing secret.

She looked through Sir Chester's trunk next, finding something she wished she hadn't seen. Hidden beneath the man's clothes were the clothes of a woman. She knew he didn't come here with a lady, so there was no reason for him to be carrying the clothes. Then when she picked up a gown and saw it was large enough to fit a man, she realized Sir Chester had a secret life as well. Now, she wished she had never snooped at all because these were secrets she didn't want to know.

* * *

CONRAD CLOSED the solar door and stepped out into the

corridor, having stopped at his chamber to pick up his dagger, after dropping off Hazel in her room. He halted and stepped back into the shadows when he saw Willow entering the solar down the hall – with both the barons, Chester and George.

"What the hell is she doing?" he grumbled under his breath. The door closed and the three of them disappeared inside the room. He took a step forward, meaning to storm the room and pull her out, but was stopped as his squire called to him from down the corridor.

"My lord? Were you coming back to the great hall for the meal?" asked Toby.

"Aye. I'll be there in a minute. I need to check on Hazel once more first."

"Shall I do that for you?"

"That would be fine. Thank you."

As soon as his squire left, he turned around again, only to see Sir Chester exit the room in a hurry. Conrad stepped back into the shadows again as the baron walked past. Then Sir George hurried out, following his friend.

"What is going on?" muttered Conrad under his breath, storming down the corridor and throwing open the door to the barons' room. Willow was down on her knees with her head buried in a trunk of clothes. "Willow!" he called out, surprising her. She jumped up and slammed the lid down on the trunk.

"Conrad. You frightened me." She held her hand to her heart. "I thought you were one of the barons. What are you doing here?"

"I'd like to ask you the same thing."

She ran over to the door and looked out briefly and then pulled him into the room and closed the door.

"Go away," she whispered. "You are going to ruin everything."

"I hope I do!" His fury grew wild. "How foolish of you to lure the barons to the room and be in here without an escort. Do you know how improper, not to mention how dangerous that is?"

"I had to do it. I am trying to find out if either of them is the thief."

"You are playing with fire. Now, I want you out of here right now."

"Nay," she said stubbornly, looking around the room and then running over to the bed and patting it down, running her hands under the blanket and pillow. "I have to check the room and their things first to see if they've hidden the ruby in here. I don't think it is either of them, but I want to be sure." She ran across the room and started going through the pockets of a cloak hanging on a hook against the wall.

"That's enough," he spat. "You have no right to go through anyone's personal belongings."

"You can help me," she said, with a nod of her head. "We only have a few minutes before they return so we need to move quickly."

"Me? We?" Conrad shook his head. "Oh, no. I am not getting involved in your devious schemes, so don't try to convince me to do so." He crossed his arms over his chest.

"Besides, Lord Beaufort already had the barons, and their room searched."

"The guards might have missed something. After all, the ruby hasn't been found yet."

"The thief is probably long gone from here."

"Nay. I don't think so. There are only a few people who knew about the ruby and where the earl was keeping it. Everyone who was in the room that night is still here at the castle, and a suspect. But once the competition is over with, it will be too late because they will all leave. I don't have much time to figure out the answer. Look for any clue at all that might tell us the barons are lying." She pushed him aside and searched a small table holding some things.

"You are crazy!" he exclaimed. "Willow, I am starting to believe that my sister's madness has worn off on you. Why are you acting so reckless? Now, stop this anon."

"Hazel's madness?" She stood up and looked at him in question. "What does that mean?"

Before he could answer, voices were heard from outside the room.

"They're back already!" she whispered, her eyes opening wide. "You've got to hide. They can't know you are in here or they will start asking questions."

"I am not hiding, nor am I leaving here without you. You are my ward until your father's return. I am responsible for you and your obnoxious, outrageous behavior."

"Fast, get in the wardrobe!" She grabbed him by the arm and pulled him into the small, adjoining room. "This is the only place I haven't checked.

"Willow, I am not –" She pulled closed the hanging curtain and left him standing there in the dark. "Bid the devil," he growled. He was about to storm out when he heard Willow talking to the barons. He couldn't leave now. If he made his presence known, how was he going to explain being in there at all? There would surely be a problem with this. Nay, he had to stay silent and wait for all of them to leave.

He heard Willow talking and laughing. It about drove him mad. He didn't want to be stuck in a wardrobe while the barons were enjoying her company. She would hear about this later. There was a crack of light coming in through the partially open curtain. He peeked out to see Willow holding a goblet of wine and flirting with both the men. That made him angry. He turned back to see that the wardrobe was empty. Still, he found himself looking in the corners and feeling atop the shelves for the ruby. Damn, Willow convinced him to help her when it was not his intent. Why did she seem to hold such power over him?

Thankfully, Willow was able to get the barons to leave. When he heard no more voices, he peeked out again to see the room was empty. He had just started across the floor when the door opened. He stopped, frozen in his tracks. Willow popped her head into the room.

"Did you find anything?" she asked.

"Where are the barons?" he said in a gruff whisper.

"Oh, they went back to the great hall to eat. They think I'm going to check on Hazel."

"I've had enough of this," he spat, taking her by the arm and leaving the room, pulling her along with him.

"Conrad, you're hurting my arm. Let go of me."

"Nay, I won't. I am not letting you out of my sight again. I don't like the game you are playing."

"It's not a game. I told you, I am trying to find the thief."

"Let's go." He hauled her back to her own chamber and walked inside to see one of Lord Beaufort's guards going through a trunk. A page and handmaiden stood next to Hazel who held on to the bedpost, her body trembling. Toby looked on from over by the window.

"What's going on here?" Conrad demanded to know.

"Lord Beaufort instructed me to search the ladies' chamber," replied the guard.

"They were all here when I came to check on Hazel," Toby explained from the other side of the room.

WILLOW'S MOUTH dropped open when she saw the guard rummaging through her trunk. "Those are my things, and you have no right to go through them," she spat.

"Interesting to hear you say that," mumbled Conrad. "It doesn't feel good, does it?" He subtly reminded her that she was no better.

"Branton?" asked Willow, seeing her friend, the personal page of Lord Beaufort in the room as well. "What is this all about?"

"Lady Willow, everyone has been searched except for

you and Lady Hazel since the earl couldn't find you two yesterday," said Branton.

"Where were you?" growled the guard, making Hazel cry.

"Stop it," shouted Conrad, going to his sister and putting his arm around her. "They were with me. And I'll not let this ridiculous behavior continue. These girls are innocent."

"The earl sent the handmaiden to search you," Branton told Willow. "She's already searched Lady Hazel."

"I do not need to be searched." The thought shocked and appalled Willow. It was so invading.

"I'm sorry, my lady, but it is Lord Beaufort's orders. If I don't obey I will be punished," said the handmaiden.

Willow didn't want to be searched but neither did she want the handmaiden to be punished because of her. Poor Hazel looked terrified, as if she were going to swoon. Willow wanted everyone out of here as quickly as possible.

"I just need to check that you are not hiding the ruby in your hose or shift," said the handmaiden.

"That's not possible since she doesn't wear any," mumbled Conrad under his breath.

"Pardon me, Lord Conrad?" asked the girl. "What did you say?"

"It was nothing of importance," said Willow glaring at Conrad. "I don't want you to get into trouble, so let's go to the wardrobe so I can be searched," she said. Afterward, she walked out into the room to hear Hazel shouting.

"Nay, don't touch my things! Those are mine. Don't touch them."

"I just have your trunk to search, and I'm finished," said the guard, opening the lid anyway.

"Leave it," ordered Conrad. "My sister doesn't have anything to hide."

"She sure doesn't act that way," said Branton.

Hazel started crying and shaking again.

"For Heaven's sake, this has got to stop." Willow hurried over to Hazel and took the girl's hands in hers. "Hazel, would it be all right if I touched your things and the guard watched over my shoulder?" she asked in a soft voice.

"I – I don't know," she said, looking up at Conrad for support. Conrad nodded to Hazel.

"It's all right," said Conrad. "We want to prove to them that you aren't hiding anything and they will leave you alone."

"I suppose so, then," agreed Hazel, hanging her head and looking at the ground.

"Move aside," commanded Willow, pushing past the guard, opening the trunk and going through Hazel's things. The guard looked over her shoulder and finally nodded, satisfied that Hazel wasn't the thief.

"That's good," he said. "I'll let Lord Beaufort and the earl know that you two have been searched and nothing has been found." The guard left with the handmaiden and Branton following. Branton stopped in the doorway and turned around.

"Lady Willow, if your cousins were here they would

have found the thief by now. Lady Fia would have noticed something out of place, and Lady Maira would have used her weapons to bring him down."

"Branton, are you insinuating that I have no skills to find the thief on my own?" asked Willow.

"I'm just saying . . . even Morag would have done something to figure it out by now."

"Get out!" she shouted, ready to throw something at the boy. Once he left, Conrad walked over to the door and held it open.

"Let's go. Both of you," he told them.

"I'm not hungry," said Willow, feeling sick at Branton's comment. Mayhap, she really had no skills at all and shouldn't have been chosen as a member of the late queen's secret group. Why did she feel stronger when she was around her cousins? Without them, she was starting to feel as insecure as Hazel right now.

"We're not going to the great hall, we are going to the secret garden," Conrad told them. "Toby, saddle the horses."

"Aye, my lord," said his squire, hurrying from the room.

"I think you both need to root around in the dirt a little to relax," Conrad told them.

"I don't want to go," said Hazel. "Please, Conrad, don't make me leave."

"It's all right, Hazel." Willow put her arm around the girl and tried to calm her so she would stop trembling. "Conrad is going with us. And he's not leaving you anywhere, so you don't need to worry."

"I want to go home," cried Hazel.

Willow looked up and her gaze interlocked with Conrad's.

"That's not possible right now," Conrad told her in a soft voice.

"Why not?" asked Hazel.

"Aye, why not?" Willow repeated, wondering what his reply would be. Hazel was insecure and always frightened. One minute she wanted to be noticed and acknowledged and the next she wanted to hide away. Willow didn't understand why she acted this way. All she knew was that when she spent time with Hazel, the girl was calm and even happy. But that would all come to an end soon. When Hazel left Castle Rothbury, Willow could only hope that the girl could be happy with Conrad as well.

"We can't leave because the competition isn't over yet," stated Conrad. "Besides, I've made a deal with Lord Rook. I must watch over Lady Willow until his return."

"And what about Hazel?" asked Willow. "Who will watch over her?"

"I want you to do it, Willow," said Hazel in a soft voice. "Please . . . don't leave me alone. I don't want to be alone."

Willow didn't know what to say. She wasn't used to being a caregiver of any kind. Neither was she good at it. But her heart went out to Hazel. Before she realized what she was saying, she agreed. "All right, Hazel, I will. I'll be with you. You don't have to be frightened anymore."

Hazel smiled, and her trembling stopped. But when Willow looked up, Conrad was frowning and shaking his head. Suddenly, she had doubts about all this. Willow was used to going where she wanted and talking to whomever she chose. She also needed to be alone with some of the nobles because she had a feeling one of them was the thief, and she wanted to prove it. She had to find a way to help Earl Alnwick because without the ruby, he was doomed. What had Willow just agreed to, and how was she going to get out of this mess?

CHAPTER 14

"It is amazing how calm Hazel gets working in the garden." Conrad took a swig of ale from the goatskin, watching his sister from the porch of Imanie's cottage. Willow was next to him, having been working in the garden for the last hour. Hazel seemed to be taking extra care of weeding and turning the soil atop Imanie's grave. The last few times they were here, Hazel spent a lot of time at the gravesite. Even Conrad had helped by digging up roots. Toby watered and took care of the horses. Willow was starting to enjoy working with the earth. The garden was regaining its beauty, just the way it looked when Imanie once cared for it. Willow could see now why it calmed Hazel's nerves and made her stop shaking. It was very relaxing.

"I don't understand what is wrong with your sister. Why does she act so . . . so . . ."

"Addled?" Conrad handed her the ale. She took a drink

as well. The day was proving to be a hot one. Willow felt sticky and uncomfortable. What she really wanted was to go back to the castle and continue her mission to find the thief.

"Has she always been that way?" asked Willow.

"She's getting worse." Conrad sat down on a wooden bench and Willow settled herself next to him. "It all started when my father died. Then, my mother became sick, and she and Hazel never talked or spent time together anymore. They became distant as time went on. Hazel turned into a recluse. My sister is a shy girl and also afraid of everything. I feel she needs to be mentored by another woman. I can't help her, Willow. I don't know how. I came to Rothbury hoping the earl would take her as his ward, but he refused. I am thankful your father is going to do it."

"I wonder why the earl refused?"

"I think he has his hands full with all the wards he has already. Some of them can prove to be quite challenging." Conrad lifted an eyebrow, nodding at her.

"Do you mean me?" Her hand flew to her chest. "I'm not the challenging one, I assure you. My cousin, Morag, is the troublesome one who is a handful. I have never caused the earl any trouble at all."

"Does Morag act like you do around the men?"

"Stop it, Conrad." Her heart dropped to hear him ask this. "When you talk like that it makes me think that you don't believe I act like a lady."

"Do you?" he challenged her, making her angry.

"I have a skill with people. I can't help it. It is just a natural thing that the men are drawn to me."

"Face it, you use your beauty to manipulate others. If you were ugly or dressed in a plain gown and hidden under a wimple, do you think you'd have the same results with others?"

"Of course, I would." She stood up and put her hands on her hips. "Sir Conrad Lochwood, you don't know me if you think that everything I do is based on my looks."

He raised the goatskin to his mouth, looking out at the garden as he replied.

"Prove it." He took a drink and swallowed.

"What did you say?" she asked, hoping she'd heard him wrong.

"I said, prove it."

Her heartbeat pounded in her ears. Never before had anyone thrown down the gauntlet like this. She didn't want anything to do with it. "I have no idea what you mean." She reached up and pulled back her hair, trying to cool her neck.

"If you want to prove to me that your beauty isn't just skin deep and that you don't use it for your own benefit, then do something about it. Get rid of the jewelry, the fancy clothes, and the face paint. Wear a plain gown and bind your hair under a wimple the way a true lady dresses. And for God's sake, wear a shift and hose and stop showing so much skin."

"Humph," she said with an aggravated release of breath from her mouth. "I don't have to prove myself to anyone, and certainly not you. Now, I'm going back to the castle with or without you, and you can't stop me." She stormed away but heard Conrad's reply from behind her.

"I didn't think you could do it, Willow, although I had hoped so."

* * *

As soon as they returned to the castle, Willow hurried up to her room to clean up. Conrad was right on her tail.

"Willow, slow down. I want to talk to you."

"I have nothing to say."

"The competition resumes in an hour. I have to get out to the field and don't want to leave you this way."

"I'll be fine, Conrad." She stopped at her door. "Don't worry about what I do."

"You'll be at the archery even as well as the joust, won't you? You said you'd watch over Hazel, so I'm hoping you will bring her with you."

"Your sister is four and ten years of age and doesn't need someone to watch over her. What she needs is a brother to let her know he cares."

"That's silly. Of course, Hazel knows."

"What do I know?" Hazel came down the corridor to join them.

"Never mind," said Conrad. "I was talking with Willow."

"Conrad, were you talking about me?" Hazel asked meekly.

"Come, Hazel. We need to prepare for the competition,

and your brother needs to go." Willow took Hazel's hand and pulled her into the room, slamming the door in Conrad's face.

"Sometimes your brother can be a real –" Willow stopped in midsentence, not wanting to upset Hazel. The competitions started in one hour. She had a lot of work to do beforehand. "Hazel, I need you to meet me down in the lists in an hour." Willow went over to the washbasin and started to clean up.

"But I thought you said we were going together."

"We will be there together. However, first I have something I need to do." Willow went to change her clothes. That is when she noticed that her heart brooch was missing. She looked on the floor and on her dresser but didn't see it anywhere. "Oh, no! I think I lost my brooch. I don't have time to look for it." She hurriedly dressed and changed her shoes, running for the door. "Hazel, you'll be all right without me, won't you?"

"I – I suppose so."

"Remember, meet me down at the lists in an hour." She opened the door and just about banged into Lord Bedivere – just the man she wanted to see.

"My lady, do slow down or you will risk the chance of running someone over," said the man.

"Lord Bedivere, how are you?" She looked back over her shoulder to see Hazel watching her. She didn't want her to tell Conrad she was talking with Bedivere. She closed the door and hooked her hand onto his arm.

"What's this?" asked Bedivere with a chuckle. "I thought

you'd be with Sir Lochwood." His eyes roamed down to her hand. She only had a short time to find out if he was the one to steal the ruby. She needed to get into his room, and she had to do it quickly. Once the competition started, it would be too late. The winners would choose their wives, and she wouldn't have the opportunity to talk to the men alone again.

"Sir Conrad has already left for the competition. I was hoping you could escort me there."

"I'd be delighted to, but what about Lady Hazel?"

"She's – she's not going," she lied. "Not feeling well again."

"The woman seems to be sickly."

"Enough about her, now tell me more about you." They headed down the corridor. Bedivere had a smile plastered on his face.

"Lord Bedivere, there you are." Branton hurried down the corridor to meet them.

"What is it, Page?" asked Bedivere.

"Lord Beaufort sent me to get you. It seems he has misplaced his signet ring. Since he and you were drinking in the great hall the last time he saw it, he wanted to know if perhaps he dropped it and you found it."

"Nay, I didn't," said Bedivere. "It seems my jeweled dagger has gone missing as well. I just came from my room and cannot find it anywhere."

"Then the thief has stolen more than just Earl Alnwick's ruby," said Willow, thinking of her heart brooch missing, too. She didn't remember taking it off, so it was either stolen or perhaps came unclasped, and she lost it in travel. It broke her heart to no longer have it and she hoped to have time to look for it later.

"Lord Bedivere, perhaps you should go help Lord Beaufort look for the ring," said Willow, trying to get him to leave. "After all, if it slid off his finger and into the rushes, you would be the one to spot it. You don't miss a thing, do you?" She added a smile and batted her eyes, trying to compliment the man. Her trick worked when he stood up straight and nodded.

"Aye, I suppose if anyone can find it, it would be me. I might have left my dagger there as well."

"I'm sure that's what it is. I will meet you in the lists if you like. Since you no longer need to compete, we can watch the games together. Mayhap we will get a chance to know each other better."

"I would like that," he said, bowing. "Until later, my lady."

As soon as the men left, Willow hurried to the solar where Lord Bedivere was staying. To her relief, the door was not locked. She scanned the corridor quickly, and when she was sure no one was watching her, she slid inside the room and closed the door. She had work to do.

* * *

"Toby, are Willow and Hazel in the lists yet?" Conrad prepared for the archery competition, feeling less than confident since this wasn't one of his stronger events. His strength was the joust that would be the last competition of the day.

"Nay, I don't see them." Toby stretched his neck and held his hand up to his eyes to block the sun.

"I don't like this. Something is wrong." Conrad paced back and forth.

"Give them time, my lord. I'm sure they'll be here."

"I hope you're right."

"Lochwood, you're up," said Sir George. "Let's see you beat my score."

With Conrad's first few shots, he managed to do well. But when he saw Hazel from his peripheral vision and Willow wasn't with her, it distracted him. He missed the target altogether on the last shot. "Damn," he spat as the crowd cheered for Sir George who had won the archery competition. Conrad threw down his bow and stormed over to the lists with Toby on his heels.

"Hazel, where is Willow?" growled Conrad. "She was supposed to be here with you."

"I don't know," said Hazel, holding her hands in front of her and staring at the ground. "She told me to meet her here right after she left with Sir Bedivere."

"She's with Bedivere?" he snapped, not wanting to hear this.

"I don't know," said Hazel softly.

"That's it. I'm putting an end to this right now. Toby, stay with Hazel until I return." He started to walk away.

"But my lord, the joust is starting soon, and you cannot miss it."

"I'll be here, mark my words. And I promise, Willow will be here with me.

* * *

WILLOW SEARCHED through Sir Bedivere's things, going quickly so she could get down to the archery competition before Conrad realized she was missing. She rummaged through his trunk and then lifted up his mattress and gasped at what she saw.

At least a dozen knives, daggers and even a few swords were hidden under the pallet. Some had curved handles, some had two-toned hilts, and one sword had a wooden hilt with at least ten notches carved into the handle.

"He's an assassin," she said aloud, shocked by what she saw. Only a man hired to kill would own so many different blades.

"Well, I see my secret is out."

She dropped the pallet and spun around to see Bedivere standing in the doorway. He walked in and closed the door behind him.

"Lord Bedivere," she said, terrified to see him there. "I thought you went down to the great hall to meet Lord Beaufort."

"I was on my way when I looked over my shoulder to see you sneaking into my room." He stalked toward her looking very dangerous. "Why are you in here, Lady Willow?"

"I – I –" She had to think up something fast or risk

getting her throat slit. Not wanting to do it, she reverted to the only skill she had. "I was hoping you'd notice I came in here. I wanted to spend some time alone with you before you chose your wife."

"So you weren't trying to steal from me?" he asked, sounding as if he didn't believe her.

"Steal from you?" She laughed and held her hand to her chest. "Of course not. I don't want to admit it, but since you caught me, I have no choice."

"Continue," he said, stopping right in front of her. Never had she felt so frightened in all her life. Here she was alone with an assassin, and no one knew she was here. There was so much commotion from the competition outside that even if she ran to the window and screamed, no one would hear her.

"I was here to seduce you," she blurted out, holding her breath and waiting to see his reaction. The stern look on his face disappeared and was replaced with a smile.

"Seduce me? Why would you do that?"

"Because I want you to choose me for your bride." It pained her to say this and nauseated her at the same time. Bedivere was the last person in the world she'd marry. She would be a nun before she was stuck with the likes of him.

"And what were you doing looking under my mattress?" he asked.

"I sat on the bed to wait for you." She tried to hide the fear in her voice. "That's when I thought I felt something sharp beneath me. Why do you have so many weapons under your mattress?"

"You were right when you said I am a hired assassin," he told her. "I had to hide the weapons there when the guards were searching for the earl's ruby. No one knows of my secret profession, and I can't let anyone spill the secret. Do you understand?"

He stepped closer and put his hands on her shoulders.

"Are you going to hurt me?" she asked.

"Nay. I don't kill women, only men. However, if you tell any man, I will have to kill him because I cannot let the secret out that I work for the crown."

"The king?" she asked in astonishment. "My cousin, Richard, hires you to kill? How could he?"

"I look out for him and fend off those who plot to kill him. I am his guardian in a way, the same as Lord Beaufort or Lord Lochwood are to you."

"I see," she said, trying to still her breathing. "Of course, I won't tell a soul."

She saw him staring at her lips and anticipated his next move, although she was powerless to stop him. He bent over and kissed her hard, forcing himself on her.

She put her hands up to his shoulders to push him away just as the door banged open and someone started shouting.

"Take your bloody hands off of her, Bedivere or I'm going to kill you, I swear I will." Conrad stood in the doorway breathing heavily as if he'd run up the stairs. With his sword gripped tightly in his hand, his jaw stayed clenched, and a vein throbbed at the side of his neck as he slowly moved forward.

"Conrad!" she cried, pushing away from Bedivere and taking a step away from him.

"Willow, what the hell is going on here?" asked Conrad.

"She came to seduce me, Lochwood. Didn't you, my lady?" asked Bedivere. With his head turned so Conrad couldn't see him, his eyes darted to the bed in a silent warning. If Willow said anything to Conrad that the man was an assassin, Bedivere would kill him. Besides, if he was working for Richard, she couldn't say anything because that might put her cousin at risk. Nay, she had no choice. She needed to stay quiet.

"I think, perhaps, it is time we head to the joust now." Willow hurried across the room and stopped beside Conrad.

"I'm not leaving before I give Bedivere a piece of my mind," Conrad told her.

"Conrad, it's fine. Now, let's go." She pulled at his arm, trying to get him to the door.

"Willow, what's this all about?"

"It's nothing, now come on." She pulled Conrad out into the corridor and all but dragged him down the hall.

"Were you really seducing him?" asked Conrad, sheathing his sword as they walked.

"Aye," she said, not breaking the pace.

"What?" He grabbed her arm to stop her. "How could you, Willow? You swore to me you weren't that way."

"I had to do something when he found me searching his room for the ruby," she whispered, looking back to make sure Bedivere wasn't listening.

"Oh. Did you find anything?" he asked.

She did, but could never tell him. Never would she endanger Conrad or anyone else's life by telling them Bedivere's secret. God's eyes, she wished now she had never gone into his room to begin with. She was finding out secrets of too many people that she wished she didn't know.

"I found out that I would never, ever consider marrying the man. Now, if we don't hurry, you are going to miss the joust. Did you win the archery competition?" she asked, hoping he had.

"Nay," he said, gritting his teeth and shaking his head. "I was too distracted by your absence to concentrate. Sir George was the winner."

"Then we'd better hurry. You only have one more chance to win and choose a wife."

"I know that. You don't need to remind me."

As they made their way to the tiltyard, Willow's stomach churned. What if Conrad didn't win the joust? And what if he did? She had been granted the ability to agree or disagree with any proposals of marriage. However, she was not sure if Conrad won if he would choose her or if he'd choose Lady Anabel or Lady Grace instead. If he chose one of them over her, she didn't think she could accept it. Conrad was the only man she wanted to wed and if she couldn't have him . . . she didn't want anyone at all.

CHAPTER 15

*W*illow watched in anticipation from the lists as Conrad prepared himself for the joust. It was down to two men now, and only one of them would win. Sir Chester was fierce with the lance, but Hazel had told her that this was Conrad's best and favorite event.

"Do you think he'll win?" Willow asked Hazel. Her fingers gripped the rail so tightly that they turned white.

"I hope not," said Hazel in a soft voice.

"What?" Willow turned and stared at the girl in confusion. "Why would you say that about your own brother?"

"I'm sorry," said Hazel, hanging her head as usual.

"Hazel, tell me why you said that. It's all right, I won't get angry." She covered Hazel's hand with hers. "Why don't you want your brother to win the joust?"

It took some coaxing, but finally Hazel told her. "I don't want Conrad to marry."

"You don't?" Willow asked. "Why not? Your brother

needs to marry. You must understand that. Every knight wants to have sons and heirs. This is important to him, especially since you have such a small family."

"I like it small," she said, still staring at the ground.

Willow's eyes narrowed as she started to understand why the girl said this. "You are afraid to be alone, aren't you? You think if Conrad takes a wife, he won't want you around."

"It's true."

"Nay, it's not! I am sure that whoever your brother marries will accept you with open arms. You need to believe that."

"I'm not well, Willow, and I know that. Conrad said he can't care for me. He will send me to an abbey if he marries. He might send me there either way."

"I'll not hear another word," said Willow. "Any woman who marries your brother will accept you and want you to live with her."

"Would you?"

That question took Willow by surprise. She didn't know how to answer. After all, Conrad had already pointed out that Hazel needed care that he couldn't give her. While Willow didn't understand what was wrong with the girl, she knew she was not the person who could help her either.

"I didn't think so," said Hazel with tears in her eyes.

Willow couldn't stand to see the girl so upset. She also didn't like the fact that Hazel felt so alone. Something inside changed and Willow realized that sometimes others' needs were more important than her own. "Yes," she answered, feeling good about her decision. "If I were Conrad's wife, I would take you in with loving arms and never turn you away. You would live with us forever, Hazel, and never have to feel unwanted or alone ever again."

"Then I want Conrad to win, and I want you to marry him. Thank you, Willow. I feel as if you are my friend." She threw herself into Willow's arms. Willow hugged her to her bosom, feeling like she made the right choice. It felt good to think about someone else's needs. However, she couldn't help but wonder if Conrad would choose her as his bride if he did win.

The crowd cheered. Willow looked up to see Sir Chester with his broken lance held high over his head. He was awarded a point. Conrad rode back to his squire shaking his head.

"Oh, no. That's not good," Willow told Hazel.

"Conrad, you have to win!" Hazel called out. Conrad turned around and looked over at the lists, having heard her. Willow smiled and waggled her fingers at him. He nodded and turned back to his squire.

"Was that Hazel yelling out?" asked Toby, handing Conrad a new lance. Conrad raised the visor on his helm and peered over at the crowd. "Aye, I think so. And Willow is waving at me."

"Hello," Toby called out, raising his hand in the air and waving back.

"Enough with the distractions." Conrad secured his shield and slapped the visor down on his helm. Then he took the lance from Toby and held the tip in the air. "I've got to concentrate. This event is my last chance to keep the other men from marrying Willow."

"But she won't marry any of them even if they choose her. That is, if she decides she doesn't want them. She's been granted that right," Toby reminded him.

"I know that, Squire. What I don't know is if she would turn any of them away."

"You'll win, Sir Conrad, I'm sure you will. And then you can claim Lady Willow as your bride."

"Perhaps," he said, no longer sure if marrying her was what he wanted. Willow was a girl who demanded the attention of every man she met. Would she ever change, or would her looks always be the most important thing to her? And would he be able to trust her? The marshal swiped the flag through the air. Conrad gripped the lance tightly as he moved toward his opponent. "Yah!" he called out to the horse, trying to focus on naught else but hitting Sir Chester's shield.

Earth flew up around him as the horses charged toward each other. Lowering the tip of his lance as they came close, Conrad smashed it into Sir Chester's shield. The tip of Conrad's lance broke, but Sir Chester remained seated. All it would take is one good blow to unseat him, and Conrad would be the winner.

"The point goes to Sir Conrad Lochwood," called out the marshal.

"Good work," cried Toby, running to meet him as he rode back to his post. "The win is as good as yours."

Conrad lifted his visor and looked over at Willow. She held on to Hazel's hand. They both looked so excited, cheering him on that he didn't want to disappoint them. Then again, he wasn't so sure he wanted to win. If so, it would put him in a very awkward position. He felt as if he were falling in love with Willow, but her actions and the way she acted around men made him leery of wanting her for his bride.

With a heavy heart, he prepared for another pass. It didn't matter, he decided. He had to win just to keep any of the other contestants from marrying her. He promised her father he would keep her away from the men. It was going to be hell enough to have to tell Lord Rook when he returned that Willow convinced Lord Beaufort to put her up as a prize bride. He wasn't looking forward to that confrontation.

"Are you ready, my lord?" asked Toby, dragging him from his thoughts.

"Aye," he said, lowering his visor and letting out a deep sigh. He had to win. He had no choice. It was his duty. He would win and then think about all of this later. But right now, he wanted this to be over.

He charged his steed toward Sir Chester, determined to make this his last pass. He was a knight. An honorable knight. He would win to keep right on a promise. He let out a bottled-up scream of frustration and lowered the tip of his lance. Then, with one mighty blow, he thrust his lance forward and unseated Sir Chester. The man flipped over backward and fell to the ground. The crowd cheered, and the marshal called out that Conrad was the winner.

It was over. He managed to secure a position as one of the winners, and now the real competition would begin to find out if one of the other two men would choose Willow as his bride.

"HE WON! CONRAD WON!" Willow shouted and jumped up and down. Then she turned and hugged Hazel.

"My brother can marry you now," said Hazel. "And then I can come live with you. I am so happy."

"Aye," said Willow, smiling and releasing a deep breath. Now, she would be Conrad's wife, and that thought made her happy. But as she watched Conrad remove his helm and dismount his horse, she realized he wasn't smiling. Something was wrong, and she didn't know what.

"Will the three winners of the competitions come forward?" called out Lord Beaufort, getting everyone's attention. "And will the three prize brides come up to join me as well?"

"Go on," Hazel urged her, looking happier than Willow had ever seen her.

"I'll escort you, my lady."

She turned to see Sir Bedivere standing there with his outstretched arm.

"Oh, there's really no need to do that." She ducked under the list and started to walk to the raised dais where Lord Beaufort and his wife, as well as Earl Alnwick, were waiting.

"It's my honor to escort you, my lady." Bedivere took her hand and slapped it onto his arm, trapping it there as he walked up to the dais at the edge of the field, nodding and smiling at the crowd.

Willow noticed Conrad scowling at her as he approached the dais.

"Ladies, please join me on the dais. Men, line up in front," instructed Lord Beaufort.

Willow hurried up the wooden stairs, standing next to Lady Anabel and Lady Grace. They both looked extremely nervous. She felt nervous as well.

"Sir Bedivere," said Beaufort. "Since you were the first winner of the games, you will choose your bride before the others."

"Thank you," said Bedivere, hurrying up the stairs and walking down the line of women, inspecting them as if he were choosing a side of beef.

"Who will be your bride?" asked Lord Beaufort.

Willow's heart thumped like wild. She kept her eyes away from him, hoping he wouldn't choose her.

"I'll take her." His hand came out, and he lifted Willow's chin. "I choose Lady Willow for my wife."

"Thank you, Sir Bedivere," said Beaufort. "But before I grant your wish, I want you to know that the late king and queen of England gave Lady Willow the choice of accepting any proposal of marriage. Do you agree to be Sir Bedivere's wife, my dear?"

Willow looked down to see Conrad standing on the ground. He stared at her intensely. His jaw was clenched, and a frown covered his face.

"Nay," she said, getting a reaction of astonishment from the crowd. "I am sorry, but I don't want to marry Sir Bedivere."

"Choose another bride, Bedivere," commanded Beaufort.

The man's dark eyes bore into her before he moved over and put his hand on Lady Anabel's shoulder. "I'll take her."

"Lady Anabel will be your wife." The crowd clapped. Lord Beaufort dismissed them. "Sir George, approach the dais. You will choose next."

Once again, the knight walked up the stairs and he, too, chose Willow.

"I'm sorry, Sir George, but I can't marry you either," she told him. Sir George then chose Lady Grace, and they exited the platform.

Last, it was Conrad's turn. That made Willow's heart flutter. She was the only one left to choose, so it was inevitable that she and Conrad would marry. Willow spied Hazel out in the crowd, looking very happy.

However, Sir Conrad didn't climb the platform. He stayed on the ground and spoke to Lord Beaufort. "I beg your forgiveness, Lord Beaufort, but I cannot marry Lady Willow."

With her smile turning into a frown, Willow's heart sank when Conrad announced that he wouldn't marry her. She looked up to realize that Hazel had disappeared.

"Lochwood, what do you mean you can't marry her?" grumbled Lord Beaufort.

"I am her guardian and promised her father I would keep her away . . . from the men."

The crowd laughed, making Willow want to hide her head and cry. She couldn't stay here any longer. Running down the stairs, she passed Conrad.

"Wait, Willow. I want to talk to you." Conrad reached out and touched her arm.

"Get your hands off of me, Conrad the Cur! I wouldn't marry you if you were the last man on earth." The crowd laughed again, and Willow felt like hiding away forever. She had to leave here and think about this situation. She didn't want to be around people right now.

Running to the stable, she bridled her horse and mounted it without using a saddle. Fleeing over the drawbridge and into the woods, she tried to get as far away from Conrad and the laughing crowd as possible.

illow approached the secret garden, riding inside and dismounting in a hurry. She needed to cry and release her pent-up emotions. She had turned down two other proposals for marriage because she was saving herself for Conrad.

But he didn't want her.

What had she done wrong? She ran to the house, throwing open the door to the cottage and stopping in her tracks. There, in the house stood, of all things, a nun!

"Oh!" she said, holding her hand to her mouth. "Who are you?"

"I'm Sister Adeline. I am here to see Imanie. Would you happen to know when she'll return?"

"You haven't seen her in a while have you?" Willow entered the cabin and cautiously approached the woman.

"Nay, I haven't," answered the nun with a smile. "I have

been away on a pilgrimage to the holy lands for over a year now."

"She's dead," Willow blurted out.

"Imanie's gone?" The woman's eyes opened wide. She reached out to touch the table, lowering herself to the chair. When she did, her traveling cape opened a little and Willow spied a heart brooch just like hers pinned to the woman's gown.

"Where did you find my pin?" Willow reached out for it, but Adeline's hand rose up to stop her.

"Your pin?" she asked, tilting her head and looking at Willow from the corner of her eyes. "I suppose I should have known you were chosen as well since you are here in the queen's secret garden."

"You – you're a member of the Followers of the Secret Heart, too?"

"I am. Who are you?"

"I am Willow. Willow Douglas. My father is Rook, one of King Edward's bastard triplets."

"Nice to meet you. I didn't think there was anyone new in the group anymore."

"Imanie trained my cousins and me, but they're not here right now."

"Why did you run in here looking so upset, Willow? Were you trying to hide from someone?"

"I suppose I was." She sat down on a chair opposite Adeline. "I was a prize bride for a competition, but I wasn't chosen."

"A prize bride? And you weren't chosen? That is surprising. You are a beautiful girl."

"Mayhap I should explain. I was chosen. Twice, actually, but I turned them down. The man I want to marry and who I thought would choose me, didn't."

"I'm sorry. Why didn't he choose you?"

"He doesn't want to marry me because he thinks I care too much about my looks and other men."

"Do you? I notice you are dressed elegantly and even have a crown on your head."

"It was the queen's crown," Willow explained. "She left it to me."

"And what about that bracelet and ring? If I'm not mistaken, those used to be Imanie's."

"You're right. I took them because I thought she'd want me to have them."

"I see. And did you offer them to anyone else? Your cousins for instance?"

"My cousins don't care about jewelry and things like that. I'm the only one who would appreciate them."

"Sometimes having less is more. The physical things in life often prove to be burdensome and get in our way."

"That's not true. I don't have that problem."

Adeline studied her face as if she didn't agree. "Don't you?"

Suddenly, Willow realized that Adeline had nothing but the clothes on her back and the brooch. She wondered about the woman. How could she be happy living this way? "What is your skill, Adeline? How are you important? Is there something you've accomplished that helped a nation or a titled noble?"

"I think everyone is just as important as another. Don't you?"

"Well, I don't know. I would think nobles are more important than servants."

"Mayhap, we are all the same in the inside."

Willow thought of Conrad's words challenging her to go without her things that made her feel beautiful. Hadn't he said he wanted her to show him she could be beautiful inside as well as out?

"My looks and my words are all I have. I am afraid because someday I know they will be gone," she admitted. "I don't feel nearly as qualified to be a follower as my cousins. Don't you see? I have very little to offer. That is why I cling to what I do have."

"Mayhap, that is what is holding you back. Perhaps it's time to change, Willow."

"Nay," she said stubbornly. "There is no reason to change now. Conrad already decided he doesn't want me."

"If you won't do it for yourself, then perhaps it's time to do it for someone else."

"What do you mean?"

"Do you know that girl who is kneeling on the ground?" Adeline nodded to the door.

Willow turned around and looked out the open door, surprised to see Hazel down on her knees at Imanie's gravesite. "What is she doing here? That is Sir Conrad's sister, Hazel."

"Is Sir Conrad the man you want to marry?"

"Aye," she admitted.

"I see." Adeline got up and walked out the door with Willow following. She went over to Hazel and put her hand on the girl's shoulder. Hazel jumped up and backed away with fear in her eyes.

"I'm not going to hurt you," Adeline told her.

"She's afraid her brother is going to send her to an abbey," said Willow. "I am sure your presence is making her feel unsettled."

"There's nothing wrong with living in an abbey," said Adeline. "I live there, and I love it. My name is Sister Adeline."

"I – I'm Hazel," said the girl, looking once again like she was going to swoon.

"Hazel, if you are afraid of something, you can talk to me." Adeline was genuine and sincere, but Hazel was leery.

"Nay. I talk only to Willow," the girl spat and ran into the house.

"Now I see clearly what your mission is, Willow." Adeline smiled. "If you'll excuse me, I'd like to pray at Imanie's grave."

"Of course." Willow didn't know what the nun meant. Wasn't her mission something of much more importance than just helping an addled girl? Surely, she was supposed to stop a war like her cousin Fia did or, mayhap, change a nobleman's decision that would help many others of her country. If only she had been able to find the earl's ruby, then she would have accomplished something worthwhile.

With the competitions being over, the earl and all the noblemen would be leaving soon.

"Willow? Hazel? Are you here?"

Willow groaned when she saw Conrad entering the secret garden atop his horse. Adeline was at her side immediately. "Is that the man you love?"

"I – I – yes. I suppose I do love Conrad."

"I will go into the house and talk to Hazel so you two can be alone."

"Nay! Don't leave me," she begged the woman. "I don't want to be alone with him. Not when I know he doesn't want me."

"Then change his mind," said Adeline wisely. "Did Imanie teach you nothing?"

"But that's not right. I shouldn't try to sway a person's mind where matters of the heart are concerned."

"Ah, so I see you did learn something after all. However, don't forget that you can change your actions and your habits and Sir Conrad will change his mind on his own."

"Thank you," said Willow.

The woman nodded and disappeared into the cottage.

"Willow, I can't find Hazel." Conrad rushed up to her, out of breath.

"Hazel is here. She is in the house with a friend of mine, Sister Adeline."

"She's with a nun?" Conrad's head snapped up and he perused the house. "I'd better go to her. She will be frantic."

"Nay, she'll be fine. Sister Adeline has a way with . . . words. And people."

"Willow, I know you are upset since I didn't choose you as my bride."

"Conrad, I'm not the same person I was when you first arrived at Castle Rothbury. I need you to know that."

"I don't know what to believe anymore."

"So then, you really don't want me?"

"It's not that," he apologized. "It's a complicated situation. Perhaps we can discuss this further, but later on."

Willow was so upset that she could no longer be with him. "Leave me alone."

"Nay. I don't want it to end this way. I need you to understand why I said I couldn't marry you."

"Well, I don't understand. And I'm sure nothing you say will make me accept your decision."

"I couldn't choose you as my bride because I vowed to protect you from men like me. I would have to make the betrothal through your father if I were going to marry you anyway."

"Men like you?" That made her wonder what he meant.

"Aye." He ran a hand through his hair in frustration. "I have to admit, I have been hard on you, but perhaps it is because I am so disappointed in myself. You see, I am no different than the barons or even Bedivere. I lust after you just as they do. That makes me question if my attraction to you is only physical or if it is deeper than that. I need to know this answer before I can make you my bride."

"Y-you do?" He almost sounded as if he might still consider marrying her after all. Perhaps, this was all a big misunderstanding. "So, you need more time," she said, trying to get him to open up and tell her more of what he was feeling.

"I guess so. It doesn't make any sense since most men marry for alliances and don't even know their betrothed until the wedding day. But I feel as if I need to find some answers first, even if those answers are only within me."

"That's what makes you different, Conrad."

"What do you mean?"

"You care." She rested her hand on his arm. "You care more than any man I've ever met."

"I thought you said I only thought of myself and that I didn't care enough about Hazel."

"I am starting to believe you do care about her after all. At first, I didn't understand, but now I think I do. You are worried about your sister."

"There is something about Hazel that I didn't tell you, Willow."

"I don't need to know."

"I think you do. One of the reasons I wanted to find someone to watch over her and mentor her was because she has more problems than just acting odd at times."

"What are you trying to say, Conrad?"

"In the past, Hazel has been known to . . . steal things."

"Steal?"

"Shhh," he said, looking toward the house. "I don't want her to hear this. I'm sure she doesn't do it for devious purposes. Actually, I don't know why she does it, but it's happened before."

"Oh, no, that's awful! Are you thinking that she might

have taken the earl's ruby and the other items that have gone missing lately?"

"I searched through her things but couldn't find evidence that would make her guilty. Has she been doing anything out of the ordinary – ordinary for her – lately?"

"Nay, not at all," said Willow, shaking her head. "She loves coming to work in the secret garden because it makes her happy. All she does is spend a lot of time digging in the earth at Imanie's grave."

Willow and Conrad looked at each other, both having the same thought at once.

"Do you think –" asked Willow.

"There's only one way to find out." Conrad hurried over to the shed and grabbed a spade and made a straight line for Imanie's grave.

"You can't dig up Imanie's grave! If we do that, we are sure to go straight to hell for disrupting the dead."

"I've been living in hell for too long now to fear it." Conrad stuck the tip of the shovel into the dirt. "But to ease your mind, I am not going to dig up her body. I doubt I'll have to dig very deep at all."

Just as he said that, the tip of the shovel hit something that sounded like metal. Willow fell to her knees and used her hands to push away the dirt at the head of Imanie's grave. Her fingers closed around a long piece of metal. She dug it out, holding it up high in the sun. It was a dagger with jewels embedded in the hilt.

"That's Bedivere's dagger that went missing," said Conrad.

Willow dropped the dagger, not wanting to touch a blade that was used by an assassin.

"What's the matter?" asked Conrad.

"Never mind. Dig some more. Faster."

As Conrad worked, Willow pulled out from the soil Lord Beaufort's signet ring and her heart brooch as well. She quickly pinned the heart on her bodice. The only thing they hadn't found was the ruby.

"Maybe the ruby's not here," said Willow.

"It's here. It's got to be. I'm going to keep digging."

When they dug so deep that Willow was sure they were going to hit Imanie's body, she made Conrad stop.

"Why don't we just ask her where she put it?" suggested Willow.

Willow removed her crown and placed it on her lap, dabbing at the perspiration on her brow from working so hard in the hot sun. When she went to put her crown back on her head, the gems winked in the light. But something was different. She wasn't sure what, but her gut told her to look closer at her crown. Sure enough, stuck into a hole in the inside metal of the headpiece was a gemstone that didn't match the rest. "There's no need to ask Hazel after all. I think I know exactly where the ruby is and where it has been all along."

CHAPTER 17

Conrad placed the stolen items on the table in the house, with Hazel, Sister Adeline, and Willow watching.

"Hazel, what do you have to say about this?" he asked his sister.

The girl looked at the items, and slowly lowered herself atop a chair. "All right, so I took them," she admitted.

"Why?" asked Conrad.

"I – I don't know why I did it." Her body began to tremble.

"Hazel, don't you realize what you've done?" asked Conrad in a firm voice. "Stealing from nobles is a crime that is not taken lightly. You could be sentenced to death for this."

"Nay!" she screamed, her eyes opening wide in fear. "I don't want to die! Please, don't let them kill me."

"Well, mayhap you should have thought of that before

you stole all these things." Conrad paced the floor, not knowing what to do. Hazel started crying hysterically.

"Now, now, dear. Don't cry." Sister Adeline sat next to Hazel, putting her arm around the girl, trying to calm her.

"I think I know why you did it," said Willow.

"No one knows why my addled sister does things. Not even her," said Conrad, throwing his hands in the air.

Hazel wept bitterly.

"Conrad, stop it," commanded Willow, putting her crown and the ruby on the table. "Your sister told me when she first arrived that she was tired of never being noticed. Hazel, did you think this would make people notice you?"

"I guess so," said Hazel, wiping a tear from her eye. "But then I got scared and didn't know what to do. That's when I buried the items, thinking no one would find them here."

"But we did find them," said Conrad. "And now that I know about this, I have no choice but to return the items and apologize to the earl and the others."

"Nay, that's no good," said Adeline. "If you do that, what is to say they won't think you were the one to steal them to begin with? Or perhaps that you knew about it all along and were working with your sister."

"That's absurd," answered Conrad. "No one would think that."

"She's right," said Willow. "We can't let anyone know that Hazel stole the items. It would ruin your reputation, Conrad. Even if they didn't blame you, she is still your sister. Plus, it would put everyone in an awkward situation. Lord Beaufort, being the host, would not be able to let this go without punishing someone for the act. It would hurt his reputation as well, and that's not fair."

"I didn't think of that," said Conrad, pacing and thinking and finally stopping in his tracks. "I've got it. I'll return the items without anyone knowing from where they came."

"Aye, we're the only ones who know the truth," said Adeline, rubbing Hazel's back. "And I won't tell a soul."

"Nay, it's not right," said Willow.

"Willow, please, don't be stubborn at a time like this." Conrad didn't want Willow objecting when they had no other options. "If you have a better idea, I'd like to hear it."

"Hazel will return the items in secret," Willow told them. "After all, she's the one who stole them and needs to redeem herself and make good on her choices and actions."

"Me?" Hazel looked up in surprise. "I don't know how to do that. I can't!"

"Aye, you can," said Willow. "And while you are returning the items one by one, the rest of us will cause a distraction, so no one will see you doing it. This is your chance to do something important. We're counting on you."

"Willow, nay," said Conrad with a shake of his head. "It's too dangerous. Hazel is not going to do it."

"Yes, I am." Hazel stood up and wiped away one last tear. "Willow is right, Conrad. I am the one who got us into this situation, and I should be the one responsible for making things right."

"Hazel, I won't hear of it," said Conrad.

"I agree with Willow and Hazel." Adeline stood up, and all three women stared a hole through him. "I am willing to help."

"So am I," said Willow. "Conrad? How about you? After all, Hazel is your sister. You should be willing to do anything at all to help her. Do you care enough about her to be a part of this plan? Don't you want Hazel to be able to right her wrongs?"

Once again, Willow had a way of using her words to get what she wanted. When she put it that way, how could he refuse? "If this doesn't work, it'll be a bigger mess than it is right now."

"But if we can pull it off," said Willow, "Hazel will have redeemed herself, and everyone will be happy their items have been returned."

"What will they say when the stolen items just happen to show up after they've been searching for them for so long?" Conrad still wasn't sure he agreed to this plan.

"Leave that to me," said Willow with a smile. "Now, do you trust me? And do you agree to help us?"

Conrad looked from face to face, knowing there was no way he could say no to his needy sister, a nun, and the woman he loved. "All right," he ground out, having no other choice and feeling as if he'd just made a deal with the devil.

* * *

WILLOW FELT NERVOUS, excited, terrified and alive all at the same time. The first thing they needed to do was to make sure Lord Beaufort found his signet ring. If so, it might be easier for everyone to accept the fact they were going to find their missing items one by one. Willow had devised a plan that included Hazel, Adeline, Conrad and herself. If things went accordingly with no mishaps, in the next hour and before the guests left the castle, they would all be happy again.

She sat at the dais table for the meal with Lord Beaufort on one side of her and Hazel on the other. Conrad was on the other side of Beaufort talking to Earl Alnwick, getting ready for his part of the plan. The meal was almost over, and the knot in Willow's stomach grew tighter. She gave Hazel the signal. She put her hand over her heart brooch and tapped her fingers on it three times. Hazel dug into her pocket, then stood up and excused herself. As she walked behind Lord Beaufort's chair, she dropped the ring into the rushes.

Hazel's eyes locked with Willow's. Willow's heart pounded in her ears. Conrad watched from the corner of his eyes, while Sister Adeline waited near the kitchen, holding back the hounds.

Hazel hurried past the nun and headed up to the earl's solar. Willow nodded at Sister Adeline next. The nun released the hounds and followed Hazel. The hounds ran straight over to the dais, stopping at Lord Beaufort's side, begging.

"Who let the hounds out?" growled Beaufort.

"The dogs just want a bite to eat." Willow eyed the ring

atop the rushes and dropped a piece of venison on the ground next to it. The dogs started fighting over the meat.

"Stop that. Stop it, I say." Lord Beaufort reached down to pull the hounds apart, and when he did, he saw the ring. "What's this?" He reached down and picked it up, brushing the clinging rushes from it. "It's my signet ring."

"Your ring?" asked Conrad, right on cue. "So it seems it wasn't stolen after all."

"Aye, you must have dropped it during one of the meals," Willow told him, fingering her heart brooch for strength.

Lord Beaufort noticed. "Lady Willow, isn't that the brooch you had stolen?" He slipped the ring on his finger.

"This?" She clasped the brooch with her palm, and her eyes met with Conrad's.

"She found it just this morning," said Conrad. "It seems the clasp must have given way because it was stuck on the . . . the . . . horse."

"Horse?" Lord Beaufort questioned while Earl Alnwick chuckled.

Willow shot Conrad a daggered look. He shrugged his shoulders.

"What Sir Conrad means is that the pin must have come off during one of my rides," said Willow, trying to sound convincing, and at the same time keep the panic hidden from her words. "Since I didn't use a saddle a few times, the pin was caught on the riding blanket."

She must have hidden the fear in her voice well because Lord Beaufort nodded and smiled. "It is good to have my ring back. Earl, I only regret that your ruby wasn't found."

"Or my dagger," mumbled Sir Bedivere from next to Conrad.

After a while, the meal ended, and the music started.

"I'll be leaving with my bride now," announced Bedivere, getting to his feet.

"Now?" Willow's eyes shot over to Conrad. It was too early. They needed to keep him there. Hazel was replacing the ruby in the earl's solar and Sister Adeline was keeping watch. The plan was that Conrad would find a reason to go back to the earl's solar with him. They weren't planning on returning Bedivere's dagger until last. If he left now, he would ruin their plans.

"I'll be leaving as well," said the earl, standing up, frowning. "It is not going to be a pleasant task telling the king I no longer have the ruby to trade in exchange for my castle."

Willow nodded to Conrad, giving him the signal. They needed to move forward quickly with their operation.

"Earl, if you don't mind, I would like to have a drink with you in your solar before you leave," said Conrad.

"His solar?" asked Lord Beaufort. "Why not right here and I will join you?"

Willow and Conrad exchanged frantic glances. This wasn't going to work.

"Lord Beaufort, I was hoping to have one dance with you before the end of the festivities," said Willow, using all her charm. "After all, you have been so kind to me, and I feel as if I have caused you so much trouble."

"Mayhap some other time," said Beaufort, getting to his feet.

"Lady Ernestine," said Willow, knowing the only way to get the man to do what she wanted at this point was to have another woman on her side. "You and your husband have been so kind to have me here at Castle Rothbury as your ward. You wouldn't mind if I danced with your husband – just one dance, would you?"

"Nay, of course not," said Ernestine, dabbing her mouth with a cloth.

"I said, not now," replied Beaufort.

"Walter," scolded Ernestine. "Your ward would like a dance with you, now do not disappoint the young lady."

Beaufort let out a sigh. "All right, but just one."

Willow nodded slightly to Conrad.

"One fast drink in your solar to send you on your way won't hold you up too long, will it?" Conrad asked Earl Alnwick.

"Well, I suppose I'll need a drink before I tell Richard the ruby is gone. Come on," said the earl with a wave of his hand. "Mayhap, we'll even make that two drinks, or three."

Willow breathed a sigh of relief, walking out to the main floor to dance with Lord Beaufort as Conrad left with the earl. Hopefully, Hazel and Sister Adeline had done their job by now.

"I don't understand why you want to dance with me," said Beaufort, taking her arm and joining the others in dance. "After all, I thought you'd want to dance with Sir Conrad before he left and that you'd want to try to convince him to marry you."

Willow kept her eyes on the door of the great hall as the musicians played a lively tune and she danced with Beaufort.

"I don't know what you mean, Lord Beaufort. After all, I cannot make anyone do something they don't want to."

"Hah!" spat Beaufort. "I know you too well to believe that, Willow."

"Sir Conrad explained to me that he will not marry me before he talks to my father, and I agreed. That is the right thing to do."

"I suppose so," he mumbled.

"Lord Beaufort, you never should have let me put myself up as a prize bride without first consulting my father."

"Why not? I figured you'd talk him into it, just like you always do with everything else."

"You weren't just trying to get rid of me, were you?"

The look in the man's eyes told her she'd figured out his motive.

"Nay, of course not. You can stay at Rothbury as long as you want."

"Rest assured, Lord Beaufort, if everything works out the way I'd like it to, I won't be your ward for much longer."

Willow saw Hazel and Sister Adeline appear in the

doorway and she breathed a sigh of relief. Then they disappeared to hide the last item – Sir Bedivere's dagger.

Next, shouting was heard. The earl ran into the great hall with Conrad right behind him. "I found it! I found my ruby." Earl Alnwick held his hand over his head, rushing in to show everyone.

"God's eyes, Alnwick, did you really find it?" Lord Beaufort raised his hand to stop the music and rushed across the hall to join him. "We looked everywhere and searched everyone. Where did you find it?"

"It was stuck under the velvet casing inside the chest," the earl explained. "I never would have seen it if Sir Conrad hadn't asked to admire the piece. He's the one who pointed out there was a bump under the velvet. I don't know how I didn't notice it before."

"That's wonderful!" exclaimed Willow, hurrying to the earl's side. "Now you can give the ruby to the king in exchange for keeping your castle."

"Aye," said Earl Alnwick, rubbing the ruby against his tunic to shine it. "And this isn't leaving my possession until I meet with the king. I won't take the chance of it disappearing again."

"I am so happy you'll be able to continue your plan of guarding the border and possibly making an alliance with the Scots," said Willow.

"Aye," answered the earl. "If John of Gaunt would have gotten hold of my castle, there would have been no chance for peace in the future, ever. This is a miracle that I found the missing ruby."

"Miracle, bah!" spat Bedivere, looking over the earl's shoulder. "It seems a little suspicious to me that all the stolen items are suddenly showing up. Don't you think so?"

"Bedivere, what are you saying?" asked Alnwick.

"I'm only saying that perhaps the thief is still here, right in the castle and only wants us to think that the items were misplaced."

"I don't believe that at all," said Conrad. "Why would a thief steal something just to give it back? That is highly improbable."

"That's right," said Willow. "So that proves they were only misplaced to begin with."

"I never, and I repeat never, misplace a weapon," Bedivere told them. "I am not that careless. Someone stole it from my room, I tell you. And when I find the culprit, I will make him pay." Bedivere stormed out of the great hall and headed toward his room.

"Conrad," Willow whispered. "We've got to stop him. There is no way Hazel has done her task yet."

"Do you think there is still a thief in Castle Rothbury?" the earl asked Lord Beaufort. Commotion started up, and the crowd seemed to go into a frenzy from Bedivere's suggestion.

"I'll take care of Bedivere," said Conrad, but Willow stopped him.

"Nay," she whispered. "You need to stay here and convince everyone it was just a coincidence the missing objects are all showing up at the same time. I'll stop Bedivere."

"I don't want you going anywhere near the man," Conrad answered.

"Don't you trust him? Or is it me you don't trust instead?"

"Willow, don't," said Conrad, clenching his jaw.

"If you believe I am not who the rumors make me out to be, then you will let me handle this, and you will stay here."

He took a moment to answer but finally nodded slightly. "Be careful," he warned her. "I don't trust the man at all. There is something about him that I don't like. He seems to be hiding something."

"I'll be careful. Now, hurry and stop this chaos before everyone thinks there is still a thief amongst us."

Willow hurried up the stairs and headed toward Sir Bedivere's solar. When she got to his room, she saw Sister Adeline trying to talk to him and distract him, but Bedivere pushed her aside and entered his room, slamming the door behind him.

"Willow," called out the nun, hurrying to meet her. "Hazel is still inside his room. She didn't have time to leave, and now he is going to discover her."

"Don't worry, I won't let him hurt her. Go down to the great hall and tell Conrad what happened."

The nun ran in the opposite direction as Willow opened the door and stepped into the room. Bedivere had Hazel cornered, and the girl had her hands behind her back and was crying.

"What are you doing?" Willow rushed over and stepped in between Hazel and Bedivere.

"I think I just caught the thief," sneered the man. "And there is no way in hell I'm going to let the wench get away with this."

CHAPTER 18

" *L* eave her alone, she's not a thief," said Willow, putting her arm around Hazel.

"I'll kill her, I swear I will," snarled Bedivere. "No one steals from me."

Hazel whimpered, and her body shook. She dropped the dagger she'd been hiding behind her back, and it clattered to the floor.

"My stolen dagger!" shouted Bedivere.

Willow saw the anger in the man's eyes and needed to do something quickly to defuse it. "Hazel, go down to the great hall, now!"

"She's not going anywhere," spat the man.

"Go now, and close the door behind you." She pushed Hazel who ran out the door, slamming it in the process.

"Now that wasn't a wise thing to do, was it?" snarled Bedivere taking a step closer. He bent down and picked up his dagger, running his fingers along the blade. "She is a thief. I'm going to make sure she pays."

"You told me you never hurt or killed a woman, or was that just a lie?"

"You know as well as I what is going on. I think Earl Alnwick and Lord Beaufort need to know there is a thief in their midst and that she's got her brother, a nun, and even you helping her cover up her horrible deeds." He turned and headed across the room with the dagger clenched in his fist.

"Go right ahead and tell them," Willow challenged him. "And then I will tell them, as well as your new bride, that you are an assassin who works for the king."

He stopped in his tracks and slowly turned around. "You wouldn't."

"Wouldn't I?"

He stalked forward, not stopping until he had her back against the wall. Leaning over, he brought his face close to hers. "Perhaps, you aren't the only one with the power of persuasion. I have ways of changing someone's mind as well." He leaned over and kissed her hard, pulling her up against his body. Willow dug her nails into his shoulders, trying to push him away, but he was much too strong.

The door banged open. Conrad burst into the room with his sword drawn. "Get your hands off my woman, or I will sever them from your body," shouted Conrad.

Bedivere spun around, holding up the dagger in front of him.

"What's going on here?" Lord Beaufort rushed in followed by the earl and a crowd of men.

Willow had to do something fast, or their whole plan will have been for naught. "Isn't it wonderful? Sir Bedivere found his missing dagger," she announced to the crowd. "It seems he misplaced it after all." She made eye contact with Conrad, silently begging him to lower his sword.

It took a moment, but Conrad must have trusted her because he went along with what she said. "Aye," answered Conrad, lowering his weapon. "That is what happened."

"Bedivere, what are you doing in here with Lady Willow?" The question came from the father of Bedivere's newly betrothed. Lady Anabel and her mother poked their heads out from behind the men to watch. "I don't like this at all. No man who is taking women to his chamber before he's even married is going to make my daughter his bride. Come, Anabel, I will find you another groom." He collected up his wife and daughter.

"Wait, it isn't what you think," Willow called out after them, but it didn't look good for her or Bedivere.

"The strumpet is at it again," mumbled one of the women as the crowd dispersed. Willow's heart dropped when she heard this. She felt the tears welling up in her eyes. When would she ever rid herself of her horrid reputation?

"No one will call Lady Willow a strumpet," Conrad shouted, stopping the crowd from leaving as he shoved his sword back in his scabbard. "I was in the room the entire time. She was never alone with Sir Bedivere."

"I don't care," called out Lady Anabel's father. "I've made my decision. My daughter will not marry Sir Bedivere after all." He hurried down the corridor with his wife and daughter in tow. The marriage was off, and Willow felt as if it were all her fault.

"If that's true, Lochwood," said Sir Chester from the crowd, "then why was your sword drawn?"

"Aye. I would like to know the answer to that as well," said Beaufort.

"Lochwood tells the truth," said Bedivere, coming to their rescue. "We were comparing the craftsmanship of our blades." His willingness to help her surprised Willow. "After all, I know a remarkable blade as well as a skilled swordsman when I see one, and Lochwood amazes me."

"I do?" asked Conrad, confused.

"Sir Bedivere, I am happy that you found your missing dagger," said Willow, taking control of the situation.

"Where was it?" asked Toby, stretching his neck to see over the crowd.

Bedivere exchanged glances with Willow and looked to the floor as he answered. "I was careless. It seems to have slipped behind my trunk. I found it when I was packing. I'd also like to apologize for my remark about a possible thief," he told Lord Beaufort. "I didn't mean for my comment to start such a ruckus. It seems after all that it was just a coincidence and none of the items were ever stolen."

"There is no harm done," said Lord Beaufort with a nod. "And since everything ended well, there is no need to discuss it any longer."

"There is one thing I need to discuss," said Conrad, making Willow's stomach clench because she was certain Conrad wasn't going to let the subject go that he'd seen Bedivere kissing her.

"What would that be?" asked Lord Beaufort.

CONRAD RELEASED a deep breath and relayed the words he should have said long ago. "I want to reverse my decision."

"What decision?" asked Earl Alnwick.

"My decision of not wanting to marry Lady Willow."

"I don't know, Lochwood," said Lord Beaufort. "Now that Lady Anabel is no longer in the running, I feel it is only fair to ask Sir Bedivere once again if he'd like to marry Lady Willow. He was the first to win a competition, so the choice is his."

"But Lady Willow already refused him," Conrad pointed out, hoping to hell Willow wouldn't change her mind and want to marry the man after all. Hadn't he just seen them kissing? What if she had feelings for Bedivere and not him? He cursed himself inwardly for refusing to marry her in the first place. Because of his mistake, he might lose her forever to a man he despised.

"Excuse me for saying so, Lord Beaufort." Bedivere sheathed his blade. "But I think Lady Willow would be better suited for someone like Lochwood."

"Marry me, Willow," said Conrad, not wanting the opportunity to pass him by again.

"Conrad? What are you saying?" asked Willow.

"I'm saying I . . . love you. I want you to be my wife."

"He wants to marry the strumpet?" asked someone from the crowd.

"Stop calling her that!" he shouted. "Lady Willow is friendly and beautiful, and because of it, people have gotten the wrong impression. She isn't a strumpet and has never been. She is a smart, witty girl with a big heart who is just as much of a virgin as that nun." He pointed to Sister Adeline who stood at the door now with Hazel.

"Well, Lady Willow, what do you have to say about marrying him?" asked Lord Beaufort.

"I love Conrad as well. Yes, I want to marry him," she answered, making Conrad very happy.

"Willow." Conrad took her hands in his. "I said I couldn't marry you before I had your father's permission, and I still won't go over his head. As soon as he returns from Scotland I will ask him for your hand in marriage. And if he agrees, I will not waste another moment. I will marry you immediately and make you my wife."

He bent over and kissed Willow in front of everyone. Someone in the crowd started clapping. Everyone joined in.

Lord Beaufort raised his hand in the air to silence the crowd. "I say we all celebrate not only the discovery of our lost items but also the betrothal of Sir Conrad Lochwood and Lady Willow. Everyone to the great hall for a celebration drink."

The crowd dispersed, leaving Conrad, Willow, and Bedivere alone in the room.

"Bedivere, you are lucky I didn't take off your head for what I saw you doing. Don't ever think of touching my betrothed again," warned Conrad.

"Don't worry, I know better than that," answered the man. "And if you'll pardon me for saying I won't be joining in the celebration toast. I'll be leaving Rothbury immediately."

"CONRAD," said Willow. "I'd like to talk to Sir Bedivere alone for a moment before he leaves."

Conrad hesitated. "It's all right," she told him. "You can leave the door open if you'd like. I'll only be a moment."

"There's no need to leave the door open," Conrad told her. "I trust you, Willow. And I will never doubt you again." He left and closed the door behind him.

"Sir Bedivere, I am sorry that you will no longer be getting married to Lady Anabel. I feel it is all my fault."

"It's all right," he said, walking over and opening his trunk, loading his things inside. "I don't think she would have made a good wife for me after all. She isn't what I was looking for."

"What kind of woman were you looking for?" asked Willow curiously.

He stood up and turned around, perusing her before he answered. "I think when I marry, it will be someone more like you, Willow."

"Like me?" She held her hand to her mouth in surprise.

"I respect you for what you did, protecting Lady Hazel."

"And I thank you for keeping her secret when you didn't have to."

"Oh, but I did have to," he said with a smile and a nod. "Because I have no doubt in my mind if I had said anything at all, you would have exposed my secret."

"We all have our secrets," said Willow, touching her heart brooch as she spoke. She headed to the door, stopping and turning back before opening it. "Would you really have forced yourself on me if Conrad hadn't come into the room?"

"Nay," he said, shaking his head. "I, too, have a horrid reputation that I don't deserve. I have to admit, I only did it because I didn't want to leave Rothbury before I knew what it was like to kiss you."

"Hopefully, you can shed your reputation someday, too, Sir Bedivere. Since Conrad said all those nice things about me in front of everyone, I don't think I'll have to worry about being called a strumpet again."

"My situation is different," he said. "And because of my secret profession, I am afraid I will never be able to open up and be honest with any woman the way I have been with you."

Willow laughed. "Now that, Sir Bedivere, I assure you only happened because I put my nose where it didn't belong."

"I'm glad you did," he said, sadness showing in his eyes. "It's a hard secret to keep and one I am not proud of, I assure you. I am almost glad you discovered it because it felt good to talk to someone about it."

"I wish I could say I was happy to listen."

"Lady Willow, you need to understand that I would do anything to protect my sovereign – the king – your cousin. But what I didn't tell you, is that he is not the only one who hires my services."

Willow raised her hand and looked the other way. "Please, I don't want to know any more. I can't say I understand why you do what you do, Sir Bedivere. But I am sure when the time comes, you will be able to change if you want to. I think I've changed since Sir Conrad came back into my life, and it is a good feeling. I only hope you can experience it, too, someday."

Bedivere smiled. "If I didn't think Lochwood would burst into the room and take off my head, I'd hug you and give you a goodbye kiss."

"Perhaps it is better if we just say goodbye and leave it at that. I wish you the best, Sir Bedivere, in whatever choices you make in your life."

"And I, the same for you."

Willow left the room feeling good about herself. She hoped that her words would help Sir Bedivere to find his path in life. But what she really hoped more than anything is that her father would agree to her marrying Conrad. Because if he didn't, she was going to have to use her powers of persuasion once again.

CHAPTER 19

A WEEK LATER

"Willow, I canna believe ye're married." Fia rocked her newborn baby, Oletha, in her arms, standing at the bottom of the dais. Her husband, Alastair, was next to her. Along with them were Fia's sister, Morag, and her cousin, Maira. Three days ago, Willow's father had returned from the Highlands bringing them with him.

"I still can't believe you traveled all the way here for my wedding." Willow looked up at Conrad and smiled. They'd just said their vows and were now husband and wife. He looked so handsome wearing his best tunic that depicted his crest of a lion and a lamb. She almost felt as if it symbolized the two of them. Although, she wasn't sure which one she'd be now that she'd changed. Although she wore one of her best gowns and her crown in honor of her late grandmother, the only jewelry she wore was her heart brooch. She wanted to show Conrad that she didn't need all the baubles because when she was with him, she felt beautiful inside as well as out. She even braided her hair and wore it up, because she didn't want anyone ever to call her loose or a strumpet again.

"Willow, you do realize that Fia didn't know we were getting married until she arrived," Conrad reminded her.

"You mean until I agreed to it," called out Rook from behind them.

"Willow, since ye didna come to Scotland to see my firstborn, I decided to come to ye," said Fia.

"I still think ye shoulda stayed put," her husband told her. "It is too soon to travel after birthin' the bairn. Here, let me hold Oletha." Alastair took the baby from Fia and cradled her in his arms. He was such a fierce Highland warrior but didn't look it when he cradled the baby and made silly voices, trying to get his daughter to smile.

"Kiss the bride," shouted Toby from behind the girls.

"Didn't I do that?" asked Conrad, teasing Willow, as if he'd forgotten about it.

Willow playfully hit him on the arm. "You heard him, Conrad. We haven't kissed since we've said our vows."

"Oh, you all want a kiss, do you?" Conrad had a devilish look in his eyes.

"Remember, I'm watching, Lochwood," growled Rook from the crowd. Willow's mother, Calliope, stood with him, having traveled here with Willow's siblings from Naward as soon as she got word about the wedding.

"We're watching, too," called out her older brothers. Willow didn't miss the fact Blaise and Jarin were really looking at all the pretty girls. Her younger brothers, Darwyn and Colton, had little interest in her wedding and were over by the well playing with a hound.

"Throw the flowers," called out Morag, moving closer to the front of the crowd.

"First the kiss," said Willow, looking up at her husband. Conrad kissed her passionately. It lingered longer than it probably should have.

"That's enough," called out Rook, clearing his throat.

"Rook, they're married now," Willow's mother reminded him.

"She'll always be my little girl," said Rook, making Willow feel emotional. "She's my only daughter so I can be protective of her," he added.

"Someday soon, I'm sure Willow will have a daughter, and then you can spoil your granddaughter as well," Calliope told her husband with a huge smile.

"She'd better not be having a baby too soon." Rook's eyebrows dipped.

Conrad chuckled and pulled Willow closer. "Don't worry, Lord Rook. I assure you that you won't have to worry. Your daughter is still a virgin."

"Conrad," said Willow, feeling exceedingly embarrassed that he said this aloud.

Willow noticed Hazel standing next to Sister Adeline.

The girl was still shy and frightened. Willow worried about her.

"Conrad, I'd like to take Hazel to live with us back to your manor house in Scarborough."

"Willow, we've talked about this. We just got married, and I don't believe we'll have the time to give her the proper attention she needs. Mayhap, it would be better for her to stay at the abbey just until we get settled."

"Is that really what you want?" she asked.

"Nay, it isn't," he admitted. "I wish more than anything that she could live with us starting now. But I don't want to put that responsibility on your shoulders. You will have enough to take care of being the lady of my manor."

"Then I'll ask Sister Adeline to come live with us to watch over Hazel until things get better. Would that be all right?"

Conrad looked out to Hazel and the nun. "She does seem to like Sister Adeline. I suppose it is all right if she wants to do it."

"Thank you, Conrad." Willow threw her arms around him and kissed him deeply.

"Throw the flowers," Morag called out impatiently. She stood at the front of the crowd.

"Morag, leave them be," scolded Maira. "Who cares about catching a bouquet?"

"I do," said Morag. "The lassie who catches it is the next one to marry."

"Who wants to marry? Not me," Maira complained.

"Hazel, look up," Willow called out to the girl. "I am

going to toss the flowers to you, so be sure to catch them."

"Me?" Hazel looked up in surprise, and her eyes lit up.

"Forget the flowers, just kiss again," yelled Toby, standing right behind Hazel.

Willow turned around and threw the bouquet of flowers over her shoulder. Conrad, as well as the crowd started laughing.

"What's so funny?" she asked, turning around to see that Toby had caught the bouquet. She started laughing as well.

"Ugh, get these away from me." Toby tossed the flowers to Maira. Maira, being the warrior she was, raised her hand to block her face. The flowers ricocheted off of her and went right into Hazel's hands.

"I caught them. I got the flowers," cried Hazel, hugging the bouquet to her chest.

"Nay, I wanted them." Morag put her hands on her hips. "Maira, why didna ye toss them to me?"

"Enough about the flowers," called out Willow's brother, Blaise. "When do we eat?"

"Everyone to the great hall for the celebration." Lord Beaufort led the way. At his request, Earl Alnwick had stayed for the celebration as well.

CONRAD COULD BARELY TAKE his eyes off Willow during the meal. The celebration was grander than he could have ever imagined. Lord Beaufort wanted only the best for his ward. And of course, Rook liked to spoil his only daughter.

Therefore, the meal consisted of three types of cheeses, both white and brown bread, stuffed swan, venison in a creamy sauce, pickled beets, watercress, frumenty pudding, and a spice cake and to finish it off, Conrad requested his favorite bilberry tarts.

"I am so full, I couldn't eat another bite." Conrad stood up with a cup of wine in his hand. "I want to propose another toast. This time, I am toasting to the two women who mean the most to me in life."

"Two?" came Rook's concerned reply.

"Let me explain." Conrad looked down the long table to Hazel who sat next to Willow. "My wife, and my sister. May they both live long, prosperous lives."

The crowd clapped and raised their goblets high.

"I'll drink to that," called out Rook. "And your life will be longer, Lochwood, now that you clarified what you meant."

"Father," said Willow. "My husband only has eyes for me."

"That's right," said Conrad. "Now, let the celebration continue."

The wedding festivities were coming to an end, and Conrad decided he would wait no longer.

"Come with me, Wife," he said, pulling her away from a conversation she was having with her cousins.

"Conrad, that was rude," she scolded him.

"Then this is going to be even ruder." He swept her up into his arms and carried her quickly toward the bedchamber.

"Oh, I see what's so important," she answered with a giggle.

Conrad got to the room and kicked open the door, kissing her and never breaking the connection as he closed the door with his foot.

"It's beautiful in here," said Willow, looking around the room.

"Your cousins insisted on preparing the room for the wedding night. You have them to thank."

WILLOW CLUNG to the neck of her new husband, feeling lucky and also aroused. The room was decorated with rose petals sprinkled across the floor and even up on the bed. A fire burned in the hearth, lighting the room in a soft glow. A dozen beeswax candles that were scented with cinnamon gave the place a spicy, exotic aroma.

"Everything is so beautiful and romantic," said Willow, feeling nervous since she and Conrad hadn't had any more intimate moments since the night they'd almost made love in Imanie's cottage.

"I don't see anything more beautiful than my new wife in my arms."

Willow wanted more than anything to make love to her new husband, but she couldn't do it before she talked with him first.

"Please, put me down, Conrad. I have something I'd like to tell you before we consummate the marriage."

"Not now, Willow. Whatever it is, it can wait until

later." He kissed her behind her ear, sending a delightful shiver of anticipation up her spine. His hot breath caressed her skin as he removed her crown and placed it on the table and started to unbraid her hair. Willow's eyes closed and her head fell back as his kisses trailed down her neck and to her chest.

"Conrad, please. I need to talk to you," she said, breathing heavily as he nipped at her breasts right through her clothes. If he kept this up, she was never going to be able to tell him about being a member of the late queen's secret group. "I don't want to have any secrets from you now that I'm your wife."

"Secrets?" He pulled back and looked at her curiously. "Willow, what kind of secrets do you mean?"

"I've been trying to tell you. See this heart brooch?"

"Aye," he said, tracing the heart with his finger. Then his finger trailed over to one breast, and he circled her nipple through her clothes, causing her to go taut.

"Conrad, I am trying to tell you I belong to a secret group."

"I know all about it," he said, unbuttoning the back of her gown, rubbing his cheek against the top of her head. "You are a Follower of the Queen's Secrets."

"Secret Hearts, and how did you know?"

"Branton told me when I first came to Rothbury." He nibbled at her earlobe as he slid the gown from her shoulders and dropped it to the ground.

"He has a big mouth," she said.

"Well, someone had to tell me."

"You're not upset about it?"

"I don't believe it is anything to worry about." His hands caressed her shoulders and slid down her arms. "You are wearing a shift?" He stepped backward and looked at her in surprise. Reaching out with two fingers he picked up the hem of her undergarment. "And you have hose on as well?"

"I am a lady, Conrad. I have changed my ways."

"Aye, but did you have to do it on our wedding night?"

"I want you to know that I won't flirt with any man but you from now on."

"I like it when you flirt with me." He reached under her shift and untied her hose.

"I'm being serious, Conrad. I want you to know that now that I am your wife, I am going to start acting more reserved. Especially around the men."

"Not too reserved. Around me, I mean." He lifted her shift over her head, leaving her naked.

"So you believe me? I thought you wanted me to prove it to you and I am not sure I have."

He spoke as he removed his weapon belt and then his clothes. "Willow, darling, I do believe that you've changed. You already proved it to me when you stopped thinking about yourself to help my sister."

"That kiss in Bedivere's chamber – that was him, not me. I was going to slap him right when you walked in."

"That, I believe," he said holding his cheek, reminding her that she had slapped him more than once.

"I am also sorry that I called you Conrad the Cur. I see now that you have changed as well."

"If you mean in regards to my sister, then yes, I believe I have changed. I told her once a week she and I will go on an outing – just the two of us."

"Oh, I'll bet she liked that."

"She did, but I don't think she liked it as much as Imanie's bracelet and ring you gave her. Sister Adeline told me she won't remove them, even to bathe."

"I thought Imanie would want her to have them. I don't need them anymore and thanks to you, I realize I never did."

"That was nice of you to give them to her, Willow. You have a big heart." Naked, he pulled her up against his body, picking her up to carry her to the bed.

"There's one more thing," she said.

He sighed and put her down. "You couldn't have told me all of this earlier?"

"I'm sorry. These are private things that I didn't want anyone else to hear, and we have been surrounded by people all day long."

"I can think of some private things I'd like to do right now." He reached around and grabbed her bottom, giving it a light squeeze.

She giggled but then continued. "Sister Adeline is a member of the queen's secret group, too," she told him.

"What?" He released her and stepped back. "A nun?"

"Didn't you see her heart brooch? I hope you don't mind since she'll be living with us in Scarborough."

"Willow, the last thing on my mind right now is a nun."

"So, you are not upset about the Followers of the Secret

Heart? My cousin's husband, Alastair, made her promise not to have anything to do with the group again."

"Is it dangerous?" he asked.

"Nay. I don't think so."

"And are you planning on leaving me to follow some unknown path?"

"Nay! I would never leave you, Conrad. You are my husband. I love you."

"I love you, too." He kissed her on the lips and continued. "Will you be honest with me and tell me everything that is going on from now on, regarding this secret group?"

"Aye, of course, I will. However, now that Imanie is dead, I don't think much will be happening at all."

"All right. Then I don't mind, Willow. You can be part of a secret group of women, even though I know about it now and it's not a secret anymore."

"Thank you," she said, throwing her arms around him and kissing him hard.

"Is that all, or is there something else you'd like to discuss, such as the color of new bed curtains at the manor house or what we'll eat for dinner as soon as we return?"

"Now you are making a mockery of me, Conrad the . . ."

"The what?" he asked, looking at her with hooded eyes.

"Conrad the Lusty," she said, running her hands over his shoulders. "Conrad the Handsome." Next, she felt his biceps and ran her hands slowly down his chest. "Conrad the Sexy." Her fingers traveled down his waist.

He took her hand and closed her fingers over his hardened length. "How about Conrad the Ready?" he asked with a chuckle.

In one motion, he swept her off her feet, depositing her atop the bed.

He caressed her breasts as he kissed her first on the lips and then covered her nipple with his mouth, using his lips and tongue to arouse her. She squirmed beneath him as he spread her legs and ever so gently entered her until she took in his full length.

He was sure to please her any way possible, and before she knew it, they had both reached their peaks and found release.

"I love you, Conrad," she cried out, pulling him close and never wanting to let go.

"I love you, Willow." He lay down next to her and pulled her into his arms. "You are my wife now in every way."

"Thank you for not being angry that I had secrets."

"The only secrets I want you to have between us from now on, are how we are going to make love next and where we are going to do it."

"But shouldn't you decide that?" she asked. "After all, you are the man."

"I think I'd like to let you decide." He kissed her again and ran a finger down her nose. "I don't mind secrets as long as they only involve the two of us and making love."

"I am afraid I might not be able to please you, Conrad."

"Oh, but how wrong you are. You have already pleased me and also have a skill like no other. I don't want you ever to lose your talent when it comes to our **Seductive Secrets.**"

I hope you enjoyed Willow and Conrad's story. I must say, Willow was a handful and not the easiest character to write. Her beauty and charm were her strengths, although sometimes they can be associated with negative connotations. We all have strengths as well as weaknesses, but all that matters, in the end, is how we choose to use them.

If you enjoyed Seductive Secrets, I would love for you to leave a review for me. Watch for Maira's story, coming next in Rebellious Secrets. Maira is the warrior of the bunch, good with weapons and not afraid to use them if need be.

Secrets of the Heart Series:
   Highland Secrets – Book 1
   Seductive Secrets – Book 2
   Rebellious Secrets – Book 3

Forgotten Secrets – Book 4

Thank you,

Elizabeth Rose

ABOUT ELIZABETH

Elizabeth Rose is a multi-published, bestselling author, writing medieval, historical, contemporary, paranormal, and western romance. Her books are available as EBooks, paperbacks, and audiobooks as well.

Her favorite characters in her works include dark, dangerous and tortured heroes, and feisty, independent heroines who know how to wield a sword. She loves writing 14th century medieval novels, and is well-known for her many series.

Her twelve-book small town contemporary series, Tarnished Saints, was inspired by incidents in her own life.

After being traditionally published, she started self-publishing, creating her own covers and book trailers on a dare from her two sons.

Elizabeth loves the outdoors. In the summertime, you can find her in her secret garden with her laptop, swinging in her hammock working on her next book. Elizabeth is a born storyteller and passionate about sharing her works with her readers.

Please visit her website at **Elizabethrosenovels.com** to

read excerpts from any of her novels and get sneak peeks at covers of upcoming books. You can follow her on **Twitter, Facebook**, **Goodreads** or **BookBub.** Be sure to sign up for her **newsletter** so you don't miss out on new releases or upcoming events.

ALSO BY ELIZABETH ROSE

Medieval

Legendary Bastards of the Crown Series

Seasons of Fortitude Series

Secrets of the Heart Series

Legacy of the Blade Series

Daughters of the Dagger Series

MadMan MacKeefe Series

Barons of the Cinque Ports Series

Second in Command Series

Holiday Knights Series

Highland Chronicles Series

Medieval/Paranormal

Elemental Magick Series

Greek Myth Fantasy Series

Tangled Tales Series

Contemporary

Tarnished Saints Series

Working Man Series

<u>Western</u>

Cowboys of the Old West Series

And more!

Please visit http://elizabethrosenovels.com

Elizabeth Rose